Brian

DALTON'S KISS BOOK 6

KATHI S. BARTON

This is a work of fiction. Names, characters, places, and incidents are products of the author's imagination or are used fictitiously and are not to be construed as real. Any resemblance to actual events, locations, organizations, or persons, living or dead, is entirely coincidental.

World Castle Publishing, LLC
Pensacola, Florida
Copyright © Kathi S. Barton 2023
Paperback ISBN: 9798891260108
eBook ISBN: 9798891260115
First Edition World Castle Publishing, LLC, July 12, 2023
http://www.worldcastlepublishing.com

Cover: Cover Designs by Karen
https://www.cover-designs-by-karen.com
Editor: Karen Fuller

Chapter 1

Ramon looked over the autopsy report that Gracie had handed him about the dad of the family that they were working with. The Croft family had lost their father and husband a few months ago and were told that his death had been an accident. However, there were a lot of discrepancies between what the pictures of the dead man showed and what the report said.

Lying it aside, he decided that he needed to take a step back from it and read something else. That was when Caiti came into his office with their son, Nathanial, screaming his head off. He could almost feel sorry for them both, but he knew he had to help Caiti before she never held their son again.

"He hates me." As soon as she handed him over

to him, he stopped screaming and looked at his mom like he was really pissed off at her. "See? Why does he hate me? I've tried everything to make him like me. I even gave him the tablet that Lizzy got him. He just doesn't want anything to do with me."

"He doesn't hate you. Do you, Nathan? Your mommy loves you to pieces." Caiti snorted and sat down as he looked at both her and their son. "You're just too tense. I told you last night when you were holding him you're simply too tense, and he knows it. You're terrified of him, and he can feel it."

"I *am* terrified of him. I'm afraid of breaking him. I mean, he only weighed six pounds something when he was born. He's so tiny. He looks even smaller in your hands. Like he's nothing but a twig." Ramon told her he was a normal size for a child. "Normal or not, the little shit hates me."

Ramon laughed. "You have to hold him at some point when he's not upset. Just don't hold him too tightly and—"

"What if I drop him?" Ramon told her that he'd been dropped once. "Well, that explains a lot. Who dropped you? Your mom? She told me that you were the perfect child. And that she wished she'd had ten more like you. I'm sort of glad that she didn't. Having only one of you is the best feeling in the world, you know. Hopefully, Nathan will not be a womanizer like your dad said that you were. By the way, I love your parents. They're amazing and friendly. And Nathan loves them."

"They love you too. Here take him and just talk to him like you do me. You know, bitchy and mean like." She glared at him but took the baby. He started puckering up the moment the exchange was made. "Just hold him like you would me."

"With my hands around his throat?" Ramon laughed. "He's already puckering up, Ramon. How does he know that I'm the one that is holding him? It just breaks my heart when he does that with his sad face and watery eyes. Here you take him. I guess I'm going to have to love him from a distance."

"It's not like you to give up so easily. Hold him. Talk to him." She said she didn't know what to say to him. "Just tell him how much you love him. How handsome he is. Just gibberish. He doesn't care."

"Hello, Nathan. Did you know that we named

you Nathanial Cooper Burke? Cooper is your grandda's middle name on your daddy's side. Nathanial was my dad's name. He's gone now, but you and I will talk about him sometime when you're older. I have pictures, too, that I can show you of when he did things, and my mom would take a picture of him. Mom was a ham, so you'll see that there are plenty of pictures of her." Ramon asked her why she didn't start telling him about them now. "Oh, I guess I can. He was a nice enough man, I suppose. My mom, she didn't like him. She did love him, but she didn't like him. She wanted to go out all the time. Parties and stuff like that. Anything and everything so long as she was in the spotlight. She'd go, but she wanted my dad to go with her, but he was never the party type of man. He was more of a stay and home in his underwear, watching whatever was on television kind of guy. But they worked it out. Dad would walk around the parties that mom would go to for a little while then he'd leave. That way, he could camp and go on hikes while she slept the morning and afternoon away. He also loved to cook out on the fire. I only know this because my granny told me about them. I don't remember either of them."

Ramon noticed that Caiti seemed to be relaxed enough that Nathan was staring at her and not crying. For a two-week-old, he seemed to be awake more than Banny's daughters. He thought his son was just about the most perfect child ever born. But he thought Banny would disagree with him painfully, so he kept his observations to himself. Ramon decided he liked his teeth right where they were. Ramon tuned Caiti out when he picked up the autopsy report.

It was right here, written out for him, but he couldn't connect it to the body pictures that had been taken at the time. Putting the photos next to the paperwork, he was able to see it now. The report and the paperwork saying that he'd been killed accidentally weren't matching up. It was as if he was looking at paperwork and pictures of two different people.

"Ramon? What are you saying?" He told her what he'd found. "Okay, but you'll have to give it to me in layman's terms. While I understand what you're saying, I have no basis to work it around in my head."

"He was murdered. Not just that, but if this is right, he had a great deal of arsenic in his body too. Enough to make it show up in high doses in his blood work. However, no one questioned it. I have to ask who performed his autopsy back then. And if we can exhume his body to have Kelly do another autopsy, that will be correct this time. You did know she was the state's medical examiner, didn't you?" He picked up the phone and put it on speaker so Caiti could hear too. He did get a kick out of the fact that she was telling the baby what a brilliant daddy he had. "Kelly? I have some information here that I need to run by you about Mr. Croft's murder. It took me awhile to figure out, but I think I might have gotten it now."

After telling her everything he had on the paperwork, he waited while she looked things up on her computer. She'd been working from home since she'd had the twins a few weeks ago, and it was nice to have her at home to contact like this. Ramon looked over at Caiti and saw that Nathan was sound asleep on her shoulder.

"You did it." She smiled at him and whispered that it was the greatest joy she'd ever had with him. "I bet. Talking to him is calming to you both. You certainly look more relaxed anyway. You could read to him calmly, and he'd enjoy hearing your voice. It doesn't matter what you say to him so long as it's not loud or tense."

She got up and then sat back down when Kelly began talking. "I can have his body exhumed as early as the day after tomorrow. It looks like the medical examiner wanted to have him cremated even before the autopsy was done on him. I'll have to look into that. I don't think they have the authority to make that decision. I could be wrong, but I don't think that I am." Neither did he. She was entirely too brilliant to not know the answer to that. "The only reason that he wasn't was because the family was dead set against it. In fact, they had to obtain a court order from the law firm they all seem to have a part of to have him turn the body over to the funeral home immediately after the autopsy was finished. They opted not to have him embalmed either. More than likely, someone was thinking outside the box and thought that it might be a fishy death. Ah, it says that Hailey Croft, his daughter was the attorney that had it written out. She's a smart cookie, that one. Sally, the sister, signed off as a witness." More keys being clicked. "All right. The order is in to have him exhumed in two days. I'm assuming that they'll want to be there."

"I'll talk to them when we get off the phone here. Also, the other paperwork, the things that we actually need to finalize the estate, are not adding up either." After telling him that she'd have someone with fresh eyes have a look at it, Kelly asked him what he'd been able to find out about Brian's parents. "Plenty, actually. None of it makes any more sense than the other issue we're all working on for the Crofts. There are a number of charge cards that are on the list of unpaid bills, but I can't find an application for them. Some of them are for a different country even. I don't see his parents having anything to do with some of these companies, either. His parents are very conservative, and these companies aren't. I'm looking into those as well to see what they supposedly had purchased."

"Let me have the name of the card companies, and I'll have a look into them. Christ, this is fun. It's adulting at its finest. I love my daughters, but it's difficult to have a conversation with them. Like Banny, sometimes, they just stare at me like I'm unglued or something." She laughed, and Caiti told her how she had just got to hold Nathan without him screaming. "I had that problem too. Banny, the know it all, told me I was too tense. I was born tense, I think."

They both laughed with her. While the two of them compared notes about having children, he looked over the rest of the paperwork that he'd been given by the Croft family. They were organized. He'd say that about them. But Ramon thought it had more to do with Hailey than any of them. Not that they were smart too, but Hailey seemed to be the one that held them all together. While Ramon had been a doctor most of the time, he'd been wandering the earth waiting on his Caiti. He'd been an attorney, too, at one point in his life. Just as he was going to put it aside, he saw something else on Brian's parents' paperwork.

"The social security numbers aren't on here. I mean, I'm reasonably sure that they have one. It would have been required at some point in their lives, I think, but there isn't one on this application." He looked through the other work he had. "None of them have one on them. And get this, I think that the signatures are all done by the same person. As in both the parents' signatures have been written by the same hand."

"Good to know. Fax them over to me if you

can. Or I can pop in and get them. Whatever works for you." He said that he'd pop into her office. "I was hoping you'd say that. I'm going to get started on this right now. Brian is working on things with his parents. I'll give him a list of things that he can look into while he's talking to them. I guess they're wanting to move here to be closer to him. Did you know that he was thinking of moving here? I didn't, but that's fine. We'll all be glad to have him around. I'll add this to the list that I'm going to give him. This is going to hit the fan badly, I think. A shit storm of shit is going to be raining on someone's head soon. I do hope that the person or persons doing this had all their paperwork filled out so that when they get their ass killed, it'll all be done for their families. I'm going to get off here. Don't forget to call the family."

"I'll do that right now." She thanked him. "I'll be there after I talk to them. If that's all right."

"Yes. That'll give me time to work on this new list." Once the call was disconnected, he called the Croft home. Since he'd never spoken to them before, he told them his name and who he was working with and then asked who he was speaking to.

"It's Hailey Croft, attorney for the family. The others are here with me. Would you mind if I put you — will this upset my mom?" Ramon told her what he was going to ask. "Yes, that would upset her. Let me ask my family, and then I'll call you back. The number that you called me on is the one I can reach you with, correct?"

"It is. It's in my office where I'm currently working." She told him she'd call him back in a few minutes. Ramon looked over the paperwork again while he was waiting. Just so that he'd have it all laid out while he spoke to her. When his phone rang, he picked it up without looking. "Slow down. Who is this again?"

"Janice. Your supposed wife's sister. When is she going to come here and bail me out." He told her that she didn't have a bail set and he wasn't going to do it anyway. "Bullshit. I want out of here. They think I'm going to sit around here waiting for them to get their thumbs out of their ass before they release me. I want you to know that I'm going to kill your wife. You, too, if you give me any shit. Where is Caitlynne? I demand that you put her on the fucking phone right now."

Janice Watson and Sam Hansberry were the much older sister and brother to his mate, Caiti. On a mission to have Caiti give them money, they'd been kicked out of the hotel and sleeping in their car. Sam had decided that he didn't want to die when Ramon showed him just how he was going to end up in a shallow grave. He had happily taken the money that had been offered to him and left the state. But Janice, for whatever reason, decided that she was going to get all the money that Caiti and he had, and nothing would happen to her. So far, she had been arrested and put in jail. With that, she was going to go to prison for all the things she'd done in the name of getting what she wanted.

"Well, aren't you pleasant to speak to? I'm sure you've been told that we're immortal. So there won't be anything that you can do to kill us, Janice. Not that you're going to get the opportunity, but I thought that I'd put that out there again. For the fiftieth time, at least. Why don't you just give it up? You'll live longer if you do that." She said that she didn't care that there were laws stating that she couldn't be killed by anyone. "Well, I guess it sucks to be you. Actually, I don't care enough about you to even care if it sucks to be you or not. I'm hanging up now. You have the life that you deserve."

Almost as soon as he disconnected the call, his phone rang again. This time he was sure to look at the number and saw that it was the Croft phone. Answering the call with his name, he got some good information from Hailey.

"My mom is all right with you giving us information. But if you could temper it a little, we'd all appreciate it." He said that he could do that. "Thank you. Also, I've put in some paperwork this afternoon that gives you full access to all the computers in the office where we all work. Mostly I'm hoping that you can get to Dick weeds computer. Oh, sorry, Brown's computer. He's a Shithead." He heard her mom telling her to be nice. "I was being nice. I didn't call him a fucking bastard."

Laughter was all around, and he had to smile. After telling them what was going on with the exhumation, he explained what he'd been able to find out about the things that weren't adding up on the autopsy report.

"Arsenic? Okay, I'm guessing that it wasn't

working fast enough for whoever murdered him. This is Alex. The oldest and only son of my parents." He thanked him for telling him that. "Also, you should know that we would like to be there when they exhume dad. Hailey, you've been speaking to her the most demanded that he not be embalmed for this very reason. We knew her reasons for it. However, at the time, I don't think any of us thought that dad had been murdered. Thankfully Hailey is the smart one in the family."

"That's what we were thinking, that someone had been thinking well out of the norm for this sort of thing. Kelly, you've spoken to her as well. She is putting the paperwork through for the work to be done. She's also looking into other things that we have on the fire on this end. But your case is high on her list of things that need her." He started to mention about the bullet hole that he found in the back of their father's head but decided that would be too much for their mother. He knew that it would be for most people. "There are some things too that I'd like for you to look into on your end if you have time. There are two insurance policies that look as if they were taken out about three months from when your father was killed. I'm having the insurance companies put things on hold for a little while. There are two different ones. I want them to tell me who the benefactor is. That will, more than anything, put a hold on the payout."

"Thank you for that, young man." She then told him her name was Olivia, the mother. "My husband wasn't perfect by any means, but he would have taken care of us when he passed. I have one policy here, too, that he and I took out after the children began to leave home. Not that we're hurting for money, but it would have been like him to have made sure there was plenty to go around. I doubt very much he would have done anything like we're finding out about having extra policies with someone else named as a benefactor. He would have, as I said, taken care of his family first and foremost."

"From the little bit that I'm finding out about him, I believe you're right. He was, according to the things I'm finding, a smart man. Someone that I think I would have loved to have worked with and to have been friends with." All of the people on the other end agreed with him. "I'll let you get back to your family.

I'll give you a call when I have a time worked out for the work to get this taken care of about his exhumation. I have a computer wizard here that will find out what's on the computer of Dick weed for you as well, Hailey."

"Great." Hailey said her name again. "If you and your family would like to stay with us, that would be great. This is a huge house, and there is plenty of room for a dozen more people. I think my mom would love to have you here too. She's been taking things pretty hard of late."

"Will you tell, I believe her name was Gracie, that I have a restraining order out on my ex-wife? Also, thank her for telling my sister to stay home for Hailey." He said that he would. And when no other information was forth coming, he decided that he'd have to talk to Gracie. "Thank you for all your help, Mr. Burke. I didn't know that my father's policy information was sent with the things that you needed. But I'm glad that it was."

"You're so very welcome." After hanging up, he leaned back in his chair to think. Again, his phone rang, and it was the Croft number that came up. When no one said anything for several seconds, he was concerned. "Hello?"

"It's Hailey. I didn't mean to send that along with the other paperwork that we gave to you. But as Alex said, I'm so happy I made that mistake. It's hard here to not become emotionally involved when it concerns your parents. I'm sure that you can understand that."

"I can. And I'm glad to help. The paperwork that you sent us about my friend's parents was enough to have us investigating all kinds of things. So I thank you for that. Without it, I don't think we'd be nearly as close to getting this figured out as we are. And we're still a long way from that." She said it was a nice trade-off. "It is. Very much so. And I'll get back to you about the time and the information about the exhumation. And I'll see what the family wants to do and how many will be coming out. We usually do things in a mob sort of way."

She laughed, and he had to smile. Hailey had a wonderful laugh. When he hung up the phone, he took what he had over to Kelly. Ramon didn't stay long, but he did look in on the babies. Yes, he thought, his son was much smarter and better looking than Banny's daughters. Laughing, he went home and called the police department to have no more calls coming to his home from Janice. He was going to put an end to that shit now. All in all, he thought it was a very productive day.

He'd figured out what was wrong with the autopsy and had settled things with the information with the Croft family. Going out there would be easy enough, he supposed, and if they got to be too much for them, he knew that finding a hotel would be easy enough.

Ramon did wonder what Gracie knew about Hailey having had to stay home. She had some freaky like powers and could see bits and pieces of the future of some people. It had to be something that had her telling Hailey to stay home, and he was just curious enough to try and track down with Gracie what had happened.

Picking up his son from the bassinet, he was glad to change not just his dirty diaper but to be able to blow kisses on his naked belly. Having been able to adopt him had been the greatest pleasure he'd had in a while, with the exception of finding his mate, Caiti and marrying her, of course. When Nathan was freshly groomed and smelling great, he took him to find his mom. Caiti was in the kitchen, but she wasn't eating.

Looking at their cook, when he noticed that Caiti seemed to be thinking hard on something, she told him that Caiti had been speaking about the baby, then frowned and just sat there. He didn't want to startle her. Whatever she was thinking about, she'd tell him when she was finished thinking. He could wait. They had a long time to work out a great many things, he thought.

Chapter 2

Brian went over the paperwork with his parents. There was plenty of it to go over too. But he had a feeling that he was talking to the wall for as much as they were paying attention to him. While happy for the little tabs on the pages that he had to discuss with them, he was disheartened about how many of them there were for him to talk about.

He loved having his parents so close. And especially out of prison for nonpayment of taxes and other things that weren't true. Millions of dollars worth of unaccountable debt that the entire kiss was looking into. However, he was getting frustrated with them in regard to the money that was supposed to be paid out by them.

They figured that since they didn't have to pay it off, thanks wholly to Banny stepping in and making it go away, that everything was finished with it. They had no reason, they thought, to worry about it any longer and wanted to get on with their lives. While he didn't blame them for that, Brian was having a hard time convincing them that they had to find out what was going on before it happened to someone else. He called his brother and sister to come to town to talk to them, and they were going to arrive in a couple of weeks. Not soon enough for him, he thought.

"Mom, you have to let me work on this. And the rest of us. Just because Banny said you didn't have to pay the money back, you're still not in the clear. Someone is out there targeting people like you and Dad. And they could do it to you again. Or other older vampires that they believe have an endless supply of money and resources could be ruined if this happened to them and they didn't look into it. If they've done this once and it worked, you can bet that they're doing it to other vampires too. You must do this for them." She said she supposed he was right, but she didn't want to be bothered with it. Dad agreed. "Well, I'm going to look into this more. As I said, it might be happening to someone else. I'd hate to think that they did this to one of my siblings and got away with it. It's just a lot of money that no one knows anything about, such as where it's going and who is collecting it."

His parents had been arrested and put into a vampire prison for nonpayment of bills, taxes and credit card debt. Well over two million dollars. That wasn't even counting the amount that they owed the bank in their town for a supposed household loan that they'd taken out to do repairs on the house. Things that the faeries who lived there took care of as soon as something needed to be repaired. He wanted to get to the bottom of this before, as he'd said to them, it happened to someone else.

Then there were the credit cards they'd been told they took out and maxed out. Not possible. While they didn't have millions to rely on, they did have enough put aside to buy whatever they wanted if the faeries didn't know how to make for them. They were being bamboozled as he'd heard Banny's granny call this predicament they were in.

"Whatever you want to do, Brian. You're a good

boy." He nearly rolled his eyes at his mom but decided he was sitting just a little too close for her not to be able to hit him. She would too. It mattered little how old he was. She'd keep him and his brothers and sister in line in any way she wanted. "We've been talking, your father and I and I think we're going to move out of the castle soon anyway. It's a wonderful home but too big for us. Why don't you get yourself a mate and have us some grandchildren and move into it? I think we're going to find us a place nearer to you here."

"Mom. You have grandchildren. Peter has three children and one on the way. Gloria has five, I think. And like me, Shawn is waiting on the right woman to come along." She patted him on the cheek. Something that he never understood why she did it and had been doing it for decades. "Why don't you want to live in the castle? It isn't too big for you at the holidays. You know that when we do go out to visit you, there is plenty of room for us all."

"I know that, but it's just too much for us. We wander around the rooms like old people. You take it. Your grandfather left it to you anyway. The others, they got some estates that he had too, but you got the castle.

You live there, and we'll come to visit." Again, the temptation to roll his eyes at her was almost too much for him to ignore. "I think that I'd enjoy living here for a change. I've had so much fun talking to Herbert and Gwyneth. I'd forgotten about how much fun we used to have when you boys hung out together."

"Mom, we've been grown men for a very long time." She told him that he was still her baby boy. "Yes, I guess I always will be. However, you do know that I'm an adult?"

"I do. But as I said, you're my baby. Also, the others, they're my babies, too, even though they're older than you by a good many years." His mom stood up and seemed to be finished with the conversation and moved out of the living room and onto the deck. His mom loved the outdoors, no matter the weather. It seemed to heal her soul like nothing else could. He looked at his dad.

"You're never going to win with her. You're aware of that, aren't you? I mean, I've been married to her since I think there were rocks around that were just tiny pebbles, and she still calls me her first love. I tell you, son, she's the best part of me, but she drives me batty at times." They both laughed but looked around to make sure that she wasn't near enough to take them to task. "She needs to, well, we both need to be getting out more. I think we've been growing mold on our backsides for some time just sitting around the house. You all come to visit whenever we call, and that's wonderful, but after you leave, we turn into couch patties."

"It's couch potatoes, Dad. I heard you talking to Gwyneth yesterday. If you'd like to go on a cruise with Mom, I'm betting you'll have a great time. It would be just what she needs after being couped up during her jail time with you." Dad told him that they were talking about that very thing last night. How he thought they'd enjoy it more since they were able to withstand the sun more. "Good. You should do it."

"As much as I'd like to, son, it's the money. We just don't have it right now, not with all this other stuff going on." He told him that he'd had a good deal of it now that they weren't required to pay that money back. "Really? You'd give it to us to go? I think that I'd like that. To take your mother on a nice boat ride. We used to do it when we were younger. Back when we had to be inside all day. But now that we're older than pebbles, we should do it again. We'd surely enjoy it a good deal better being about to be out and about like we are here. By golly, I think we will. You'll help me with that, won't you, son? I'd like that."

"Yes, but I think you should ask Gwyneth about which trip to go on and what you'll need to do when on the ship. She's a pro at it. She might even know which cruise line to take and a trip that you might enjoy the most." Dad stood up. "Are you leaving today?"

"No. But I'm about as excited about this as I have been anything for a while. Goodness, son. We'll do it. By golly, yes, we will." Dad went out on the deck to talk to Mom.

He'd bet by this time next week, they'd be gone on a long cruise and having the time of their lives. He'd be stuck here working on seeing how they'd been taken advantage of and wondering over and over why he didn't go with them.

If they left soon, Brian knew he'd have to call his family and tell them to hold off on coming. Or maybe not. He'd love to hang out with them for a while, just on his own. Going to find Banny, he loved that everyone was calling him that now instead of Bancroft, he asked him if he had any plans for the evening. Banny asked him what he had in mind.

"Dinner. With us boys, as my mom calls us. I'm going to see if my brother can pop in and be with us as well." They both laughed. "Also, you might want to warn your grandma. I think that my parents are going to needle her to death about cruises. Banny, are you sure that we won't have to pay that money to the bank? If we might end up having to do that, I'm going to need to borrow some money from you. Of course, I'll pay you back, but I just promised my parents that I'd foot the bill for this cruise."

"Don't worry about that. I think that they need this more than anything. I'm glad that you suggested that for them. And no, you're not going to have to pay anyone anything." Brian told him that he owed him. "It's my pleasure to help you out with this. I just wish you'd have come to me sooner."

"I was embarrassed if you want to know the truth." Banny told him that he could understand that as well. But not to do it again. He should know him better than that. "I won't. I just hope someone else doesn't have to come to you about this stuff when they target someone else. And I thank you very much for your help."

"You're my friend, Brian. You have been forever like the others. I'm so happy that we could all be there for each other when we need each other. Now all we have to do is find your mate, and everything in the world will be perfect." Brian rolled his eyes at his friend and then looked around for his mom. The two of them laughed when he told him he was afraid of his mother. "To be honest with you, Brian. I'm terrified of all the women in this family. Especially Kelly. She might not ever curse, but she can make you feel about an inch tall when she's upset with you. Kelly won't even raise her voice when she's giving you a good dressing down."

"Then I suggest that you don't upset her. Moron." Again, they laughed. It was, he thought, the most he'd laughed in a long time, and it felt great. "Dinner tonight, and then we'll work on the projects you have going on in the morning. There are a couple of things that I need to finish up with my job, but that won't take all that long. Being a consultant for businesses has been nice, but I'm getting bored with telling people the same thing every time. Expand. No one wants to do that. They only want to repair and do things the way they've been doing since their great-great grandda had been doing it."

"Getting people to do that has been difficult for me as well. It's like they think that times haven't changed enough for them to do much more than their grandfathers did before them." Brian just shook his head while agreeing with him. "But we can only do so much before we just have to walk away. I'm assuming that's what you're thinking of doing."

"Yes. More so since coming out here. I can do my job from anywhere and be home nightly if I want. But it's, as I said, boring." Brian asked him if he had anything that he could do within his business ventures. "You don't have to pay me, but I've learned that I can get into a great deal of trouble if I'm not busy all the time."

"You and me both." They both laughed, and he told him that he'd contacted his brothers, and they were all for popping in to have dinner with him and Kelly. It would be a good night doing something that he'd not done in a good long time. Just having some fun with the family.

They were all free to have dinner, as it turned out. The women were going to order Chinese food and pig out on it tonight at Banny's home. He was glad that everyone seemed to get along so well and was happy to have such close friends as he did. It made life a little easier to take, especially being around as long as he and the others had been.

Dinner was fun. They all put their cell phones in their cars and didn't talk about anything but memories of growing up together. The things that were brought up were great memories too. He'd forgotten about most of them. It was fun for him to hang out with the five of them without the wives. While he loved their mates as much as he did his own sister, he was thrilled beyond words that he could talk to any of them, and they'd not treat him any differently than he thought their own brother. If they had one.

Since he'd been staying with Banny, he was getting lazy about getting his own place. Brian thought that he needed to get him his own place to live in so he'd have a place to call his own. He didn't want to go back home, and he just decided that he'd take the castle, but he'd not live there full time. It was too remote from people, and he decided that he needed it more than anything right now. Not that Banny had ever made him feel unwelcome, he knew that he needed a place to go to where he could do what he wanted.

A house to hold his family too. Big enough that they'd not be all over each other when they visited. He was hoping that he could convince his parents to stay with him, but he knew that they wanted their own place as well. They'd been alone for a while longer than he'd been, and they'd like that more than anything. The quiet time. He told his friends and family what he'd been thinking. Clyde spoke about homes that he had around town.

"I have a couple of houses near us that are up for sale. One of them is about what I think you're wanting. Eleven bedrooms that aren't all crunched up together. There is a nice pool with a pool house. Also, if I remember correctly, there is also a butler's home. That would be perfect for your parents to have their own place to go." He asked him if they could go see it tomorrow. "Yes. I have things to do in the morning, but I'm free after that. I'll call the realtor tomorrow morning to set something up."

"Thanks, Clyde. I appreciate that." Banny told him that he'd need to get himself a faerie. "Why? I mean, I don't mind, but why do you think I'll need one? I know that my parents have had a few at the castle, but no one has ever been assigned to me specifically."

"They can have the house finished before your family moves in with you until they find their own homes. And I mean stocked with food too. That'll make it so they don't feel like they need to get a hotel. They're more than welcome to stay at our house while here, but if you have the room, they'll enjoy that more, don't you think?" Brian nodded. Then told Clyde he was on a tight budget. "We can work something out. Just go look at the house keeping in mind how many memories you can make while living there."

"That would be wonderful, especially for my siblings. They have kids, so I'm not sure how much they'll like bothering you. I know you won't be, but they'd feel that way." Banny told him he could understand that too. "You know, I don't know how I was lucky enough to find such friends as you guys are. And I simply love your wives. I'm glad that they're not mine, but I do love them."

They laughed about a great many things that night. When the restaurant was close to closing, they left the place. Standing out in the late night, the six of them hugged each other tightly before going their separate ways. Christ, he did love them like they were all blood-related. And he'd do anything in the world for them, too, as he knew they'd do the same for him. As he was headed home, he thought about the house that Clyde had spoken about and made his way there. He'd not break in, but he wanted to see it, to make his night a little easier in dreaming up what it might look like.

~*~

Hailey was ready to not just quit her job but to shut down the entire law firm and start again. She had no idea what her dad had been thinking when he took on Everett Brown as an attorney, but the Shithead was bouncing on her last nerve, and she'd had enough. When her desk phone rang, she almost didn't answer it. When she did, it put a smile on her face so quickly that she wondered where her head was if a call from a near stranger could have such an effect on her wellbeing.

She told Gracie what she'd been thinking.

"Good. That might go over better than what we've been finding out about your troublemaker. By the way, are you feeling better?" Hailey thought of two things that had happened to her the day Gracie told her to stay home with her sister. Her dog had died, it still brought her to tears when she thought of finding him and the accident that had happened at the exact time and location that she would have been on her way to work that morning. Four people had been killed, and three others were still in the hospital from their injuries. She told Gracie that she still thought about the things that she'd missed, as well as missing her dog. "I've never had a pet myself, always trying to keep one step ahead of shit going on. But I have known people that have had them. It hurts as bad as losing a child, I've been told."

"It does. Even though I've never had any children, I do have nieces and nephews. I don't know what I'd do if something was to happen to them." Hailey felt her eyes fill with tears and wiped at them. "I'm sorry. It's been a rough morning so far, and it's only nine-thirty."

"Can you talk?" Could she? After telling her that she was going to close her door, Gracie asked her to go to the wipe-off board in her office instead of going back to her desk. "On the left upper corner of your office wipe-off board is a camera complete with sound and color. If you would allow me to pop into your office, I can take care that you're not recorded or heard from now on, no matter where you go."

She could only stare at the device now that she knew it was there. When Gracie was suddenly in the room with her, she noticed that she was careful to stay out of the camera's view as well. With a snap of her fingers, the device was still there, and she looked at the other woman.

"I'm a wizard. One with considerable powers and magic. I can do things that no one else can do, like finding the cameras and other devices that are planted all over this building. As of now, none of them work. All right?" Hailey nodded. "You're freaked the fuck out, aren't you?"

"Yes." She looked around her office with the eye for looking for other devices that were put in her office. While she didn't see anything, she had a feeling that they were all over her office still. Hailey turned and looked at Gracie. "Shithead did this, didn't he?"

"He ordered it done, but he didn't actually do it." Hailey asked her what the difference was. "Shithead has three of your junior attorneys doing his bidding with the hopes that when he takes over, he'll make them a full partner. I'm going to have a talk with them tonight when they're home. I have to take care that their homes are taken care of as well as I have this building. Brown is going to be majorly pissed when he figures out that he can no longer see nor hear you. I'm giving you that heads up so that when he comes here, and he will, you'll be prepared. He's blackmailing other attorneys, too, just so you know."

"Why? I mean, why is he working so hard to get me out of this office?" Shaking her head, it occurred to her why. "He wants the firm. I mean, if I were that stupid, I guess that's what I'd be doing too. Does he really think that I'm just going to walk away from here? My grandda built this firm along with the building decades ago. We have a good standing as a good law firm here. What does he hope to gain by doing this to me, to us?"

"Money? The firm's name? It could be any number of things that he has in his head right now. I do know, as I told you before, that he did kill your father. How? He not only poisoned him—as you have already pointed out, it must not have been working fast enough for him. But he did shoot him in the back of the head. He paid out a great deal of money to—by the way, he can no longer get into the firm's account. Nor the petty cash. He nearly drained the petty cash in order to have the firm pay for the cameras as well as the poison that he used on your dad. I've found his stash and put most of it back." Staggering to her desk, she sat down. When that wasn't working for her, she put her head between her knees. "You're going to be all right, Hailey. All of your family will be. I promise you."

"It won't bring my dad back, and that's all I really want." When the touch of her hand warmed her arm, Hailey could finally sit up. She looked at Gracie. "I have a feeling that the Bancroft Kiss is a great deal unlike others that are around. I'm thinking, just because I've seen you, that they're all pretty strong magically. Am I right?"

"Yes, we are. Moreso than anyone can imagine right now." When nothing more was said, Hailey didn't know what to think. When Gracie turned towards the doorway, she smiled at her. "He won't be able to see me nor hear me when I speak to you. Just answer his questions, and I'll help you with what to say to him. All right?"

Before she could ask Gracie what was going on, Shithead opened her door and came into her office like he owned it. When he glanced at the area where the camera was, Gracie told her to ask him what he was looking for.

Hailey sat back in her chair and glared at Shithead. "What are you looking for?" That question startled the man, and Gracie told her good job.

"Looking for? Nothing. I was just...I thought that I saw something there. What are you doing here today? I thought that you'd lost your cat or something and were too distraught to come into work today." She told him that was days ago and that it was her dog. Taking her cues from Gracie, she asked him what he wanted. "I don't need to have a reason to come into any place I please, Ms. Croft. You'll do well to remember that. And when the will is read, then we'll see who is in charge of this place, won't we? And in the event that you don't know it already, I'm going to terminate you and the rest of your know-it-all family."

"The will was read two days ago. Not that I see that that's any of your business. Since you weren't in it, I guess there wasn't any reason for you to have been there." He looked shocked. "However, the attorneys that my dad had to draw up his will are confused about the second will supposedly of my dad's showing up about six months ago at the courthouse. They're looking into that, by the way. Is that about the time you started to give him arsenic in his tea? Or had you been working on killing him off before that? However you come up with this stupid plan of yours to fire us, you're not in charge. Never will be either."

Brown had never looked so pale in all the time she'd seen him. He was already a sickly-looking man to her. So when he reached for the chair as if he might fall over, she asked him what he was upset about. He took his time answering her, and Gracie was still laughing when he told her that he thought he'd be notified of the reading of the will since they were good friends.

"I don't think my father thought of you as anything more than a partner in the firm. Or even if he thought of you at all. I do know, from helping my dad, that he was looking for a way to get you out of here to no longer have you as anything in his firm. And it was his firm despite what you think. Now it's mine. I'm going to continue my work on that as the days go forward too. I want you out of here." He told her she was a liar. "No. I'm not. I'm thinking, however, you are. Did he know the lengths that you — well, of course, he did. You shot him in the head, didn't you? In the back, so I'm wondering if he had any kind of inkling as to how far you'd go to harm my family. Are you forever taking the coward's way out?"

"You don't know what you're talking about. I had nothing — your father and I were friends." Hailey stood up and said that she was the liar again. "I'm going to have you disbarred and out of this firm, Hailey Croft. You've been nothing but a pain in my ass since the day I was hired."

"I'm glad that you remember that I was here before you and will be here long after you're gone. This is the Croft & Croft firm, not Croft & Brown. And I'm going to do everything in my power to make sure that you go down for the murder of the most wonderful man I ever knew." She started to walk around her desk and hit the man when Gracie told her to stay still. With a quick glance at her, she saw that not only was Gracie standing up, but she was glowing.

"I'm going to protect you with all that I am, Hailey, but this isn't the time for you to get physical with him. He's pissed and dangerous right now. Also, just so you're aware, you've been poisoned, as well as your brother. You both have been rid of it, but I'd not partake of anything ever offered to you from here again." She looked at Gracie then, and so did Shithead. Although he couldn't see Gracie, she could. And it was the scariest smile she'd ever seen on another person's face before. "I'm going to make him leave here. I want you to have a seat in your chair and pretend as best you can that nothing he's said bothers you."

Sitting down wasn't that difficult. She was weak in the knees by then and needed to sit down. Knowing that he'd tried to kill her and her brother scared her to no end. Picking up her pen, Hailey was proud of herself that her hand didn't shake. Every other part of her body was spent right now, and it was all she could do not to burst into tears.

Hailey wasn't sure how she ended up at her apartment, but she was glad that she was there. Gracie sat across from her, not saying anything while she cried her heart out. Her dad, her hero, was gone, and there was a bastard in the offices trying to kill her and Alex off too. She wondered if anything was going to be all right again.

Waking up on the sofa, she wondered how she'd been able to fall asleep. She'd barely been sleeping since her father had been murdered and felt refreshed when she stood up. Gracie was in the kitchen talking to someone when she came out of the bathroom. Walking into the tiny area, she was confused when she didn't see anyone else in the room with her.

"This is Dagwood. He's been telling me about Shithead and what he's been up to since you left." Hailey didn't see anyone and said as much to Gracie. "Oh. He's little. Dag, make yourself known to her so that you two can get together. He's going to be staying with you."

The little man hovered in front of her. While she'd

not been aware of that many otherworldly creatures, she would never have believed that there were little people. Faerie, she supposed he'd be called. Just to be sure, she asked him what he was. The man looked as if he might pop a button or two on his little vest when she told him that he was quite handsome.

"Thank you, my lady. Thank you indeed." He bowed before her when she put out her hand for him to land on. "I'm your faerie, my lady. I'll be with you for the rest of your days if you'll allow it. Not in the bathroom nor your bed chambers unless you call for me. Then I'll be there, Johnny, on the spot for you."

"Thank you." She looked at Gracie. "I don't want to sound ungrateful, but why is Dagwood going to be staying with me?"

"He'll protect you. CJ, you've not met her as yet. She's the faerie queen. She decided that you'd be better off with a faerie to call upon in the event that Shithead gets stupider. And he will as the days go on. Which, as you more than likely understand, will make him stupider." Nodding, she sat when Gracie gave her a cup of tea. She didn't care for tea itself, but she did stir it while she listened to Gracie. "Dag, tell her what has been going on since she left today."

"Oh well, that man was in a rage, you see. Tore up his office from one end to the other." He shook his head like he was still in disbelief. "But he's more upset that he can no longer get in touch with the men and woman that he had blackened into doing his bidding. Lady Gracie took care that they're getting paid while they hide out from him. Monster of a man if you ask me." Gracie corrected his term of blackmailing, not blackening someone. "I'm sorry, miss. I am an old man and forget the terms sometimes."

"Don't worry about it, Dag. It's all good." Gracie turned and looked at her then. "The three people that work for you are currently writing out statements for the police as to what they were made to do. Ms. Baker, she's your secretary, I believe, she wasn't wanting to be a partner in his dirty deeds, but he was blackmailing her because he told her that you'd fire her when you found out that she was a lesbo, his word, not mine." Hailey said that she didn't care what she was so long as she did her job. "Yes, I believe that is what she was told by your brother Alex. He's helping the police while they do research. His office was bugged as well."

"Yes, bugged but not by my kind, you know." Gracie just shook her head when Dag seemed to have the need to clarify that. "There are all kinds of bits and pieces that the investigators are finding. They're going over the books too though I don't know entirely what that means."

"They're searching the books that have to do with debit and credits of the firm. Do you know if they've found out much?" Gracie nodded and said that they had found plenty but weren't telling anyone just yet. "That can't be good. All right. What else do I need to know? I'm assuming that the rest of your family will be here sometime tomorrow. Mom is excited to have company. She said that the house was simply too big and held too many memories for her right now. It'll be good that she'll be able to make new ones."

"I've told you about everything that I'm aware of. Well, nearly all of it. Also, your mom, she's a good deal like you, or you're like her, I guess. She has it in her head that Shithead killed your father and how. But she's not asked anyone yet. I'd wait if I were you until she asks. I think she'll handle it better by getting bits and pieces on her own. For now, at least." Hailey agreed with Gracie. "I'm not sure how much more you can take right now, but I do want to let you know that I've made you immortal. Your family as well. While I can see parts of your future, I can't see it all. I do know that Brian Tessler, a vampire of good standing, is your mate. Do you have any questions about that?"

Hailey could only stare at her. For a full five minutes, neither of them said a word. When Gracie sat down at the table, indicating that she should join her, Hailey decided that she'd rather be up and on her feet. Having no idea why, as Gracie had never hurt her before, but she wanted to be able to dodge whatever came next. Then she asked if she was all right.

"No. I mean, I think so, then you said that. While I have an idea what a mate is, something like a partner for life, I'm not sure how much I can devote to anyone other than my — what the hell am I saying? I don't have time for this sort of shit." Gracie laughed. "This isn't a laughing matter in the event that you didn't get that. I really don't have time for someone who thinks that I'm going to be at their beck and call. Do vampires — I'm assuming that he's a vampire like the others are." It occurred to her that she'd told her that, but her mind was in a whirlwind right now.

"He is. A good man too. His parents, unlike the others, are still around. Nice people as well. He has family as well as issues that he's currently dealing with for them." Hailey didn't know what to say or even to ask. "It'll be better for you in the long run, Hailey, to have not just a mate there for you but the strength and power of the kiss. Banny, the kiss's king, is a great man. I bust his chops all the time, but he's a good vampire and one that can be depended on to do the right thing when necessary."

"I don't need anything else on my plate right now, Gracie. I'm barely hanging on as it is." She said that Brian would help her with that. That mates balanced each other. "I don't know what to think. Or what to do. I have this bastard trying to kill my brother and me. He's already killed my dad. Then you tell me that I have a mate. With a man that I don't know. Who is a vampire. Not that I have a problem with him being a vampire, but it does bring up all kinds of shit that I'm not ready for right now. Is the sex as good as they say it is?"

Gracie laughed at the question, earning a glare

from Hailey. "More so." Gracie stood up and left the kitchen. "I'm going to go home. I thought that if I were to pop out of the kitchen right now, you'd have a heart attack, so I'm going to take myself out of doors to leave."

"You know that doesn't help at all." Gracie laughed. It was a good laugh, a laughter that she thought the woman used a great deal.

Chapter 3

Brian leaned against his borrowed car and thought about the house he was looking at right now. It was a good deal bigger than he'd thought it would be. Though why he'd thought that it would be small was beyond him. He'd been told it had eleven bedrooms. He was getting ready to walk around the property when he suddenly saw someone standing on the steps.

From behind, he could tell she was female. Her long hair, hanging well past her hips looked shiny and incredibly soft. He found himself wanting to take a hank of it to his skin to see if it was as soft as it looked. Brian just knew that her eyes were going to be dark brown.

When she turned around, he stood up to see

who it was when she turned around to look at him. She looked terribly confused. Brian took another step when she put up her hand. Stopping, he asked her if she was here to look at the house too. He'd been wrong about her eyes. They were a brilliant shade of blue, almost clear in color.

"My name is Hailey Croft. I don't know that you know me nor I you. But Gracie, she told me that you were my mate." He nodded but stayed where he was. "I was in my kitchen just now and thinking about how I'd like to just get away for a few minutes. Then I thought of you and what you might be doing. The next thing I know, I'm standing here with you. I'm trying very hard not to pass out, so you know."

"Don't do that. The distance between us isn't far, but I wouldn't want you to bump your lovely head on the step if I didn't make it." Nodding, she looked at the car pulling into the driveway. Brian turned to look, then looked back at Hailey. "That would be the realtor. Joan. She's going to show me, well, us now, the house to see if it's something that we can live in. Are you all right with that?"

"I don't know what the fuck I'm all right with or

not right now." He smiled, making sure that he didn't laugh at her. She did look very freaked out. "Will you not jump me or anything just now? I don't know that I can handle anything else right now. I'm stressed about as far as a person could be without having a stroke or something."

"I promise not to jump you until you say it's all right." She cocked her head at him, and he did laugh then. "You're very cute when you're stressed. Has anyone ever told you that before?"

"I don't know that I've ever been called cute. At least not since I was a toddler." Joan came up to him, and he was thrilled when Hailey came toward him. Taking a chance of getting himself into trouble, he introduced Hailey to Joan. "This is my wife, Hailey Croft Tessler. We're going to look through the house together."

"Oh." Joan seemed confused. He wasn't sure if it was because of Hailey or them going to be going through the house. "Well, here is the paperwork for the house. Everything has been filled out, and as soon as you both sign the last page, I'll have this filed away."

Hailey took the paperwork and then handed it

to him. "This says that we own this house. That the two of us have received this house as a gift from Clyde and Gracie Williams. I thought you were here to show us the house." Brian looked over the paperwork and then found the note at the back of the file. It was from Clyde.

Handing it over to Hailey, he told Joan that they had everything that they needed and would be getting in touch with Clyde soon. Also that he'd drop the signed paperwork off at her office later today. Making her leave them, using a bit of his magic, Joan was in her car and out of sight in a few minutes. Leaning against the car again, he watched as she read over the note. Mostly to see if she could.

"I don't understand. He gave you…well, us this house three days ago. Gracie only told me today that you were my mate." He said that he'd not been made aware of her being her mate until she told him. "I'm confused as to why someone would do this. I don't know them well enough for them to be just handing over a huge fucking house."

"But he does know me. We've been friends for a very long time." He pulled out the specs on the house and put the rest of the paperwork in his car. Putting out his hand, he smiled at her. "Well, Mrs. Tessler, would you like to go through the house with me? I think it might be a great deal of fun to see what it has in store for us."

"I'm not going to let you rule me." He started to tell her that he had no intentions of doing anything like that when she spoke again. "I'm sorry. That was uncalled for, and I don't know you well enough to have accused you of anything. You don't know me any more than I do you, and I'd love to go through the house with you."

She took his hand into hers, and they started for the house. Just as he was trying to think of a way to gently tell her that she had read a very old and select language of vampires, she stopped and turned to him again.

"I don't know what to think or do. One minute I'm in my kitchen, cleaning up the mess I made when I dropped a teacup and saucer that I'd never seen before then I'm standing here. And there you are. Is this some of the magic that Gracie might have given me when she touched me? I have a feeling that's all it would take from her." Brian told her that she might well have gotten some from him as well since she accepted him as her mate. "I see. So there isn't a need for us to get sexual for me to be safe."

"I didn't say that. You will be safe so long as I'm around. However, you'll be stronger on your own after we get 'sexual.' But I'm not going to rush you into anything." She said that she hoped he'd not do that. "I promise you, Hailey, I won't do anything that you don't ask me for."

The door to the house swung open as the two of them stepped up on the wrap-around deck. As soon as they took the first step over the threshold, putting their foot down at the same time, Brian felt warmth. Then... nothing.

Brian sat up on a bed in a room that he'd never been in before. When his head began to spin, he laid back down and counted to ten three times before he didn't think he was going to throw up. Sitting up slower, taking his time to let his head adjust, he remembered that he was with Hailey and looked around the room for her. Of course, he thought, it made him ill again.

"I'm here." He asked her where here was when

she spoke to him. *"We're in the house that we were – the one that we own, I guess."*

"So I'm in one of the many bedrooms. How on earth did you get me up here?" Hailey told him as she was coming into the room that the faeries had done it for her. "Are you all right? I feel like I've been hit in the head several times."

"You did, apparently. When the house accepted us, that's what I was told had happened. The power that it has, yes, the house has power, blew us back with its excitement." She sat on the bed and handed him what looked like a thicker file than he'd had for the house. "This house was filled with faeries for centuries, I was told. Humans have never been able to buy the house because the magic in it was overwhelming to them. Not that they knew what it was about it, but that's what I was told by one of the millions of faeries that live here. They'd practice their magic in here with each other so that they could perfect it. I don't know why a house, but it was working for them, so they didn't change things as the centuries went by. However, they did upgrade things when they saw what other homes looked like while working around. When the house needed to be repaired at times, they made it so that the house could protect itself with its own magic."

"The house was protecting itself from us?" She said she didn't think she was explaining it right and called for someone named Dag. When the little man arrived, he had another faerie with him. "I'm assuming that you were given Dag, and now I'm going to have a faerie too."

"Yes. Don't ask me why. I beg of you. If I have one more person explain to me the needs of a faerie, I'm going to go back home. Which I can do. I also found out that the note that you handed me was in another language. Vampire." He nodded and said he was going to talk to her about that. "Yes, then the house got all happy and blew us into the yard. I'm not upset. I was at first, but I'm not now. In the house's excitement, as I said, it was too powerful in its happiness that we were here, and that's what blew us back. He's, I think the house is a he, he's very sorry now and is hoping to make it up to us. I'm not entirely sure how that would work, but he's been looking in our minds to fill out the home for us. The yard too. It's lovely now. Did you know that we have a pool and an extra house called a butler home?"

If he was honest, he was slightly overwhelmed by Hailey. She was talking a mile a minute right now, and he didn't know her well enough to know if she was just talking like this because she was nervous or she spoke fast all the time. Brian knew that he'd get used to it. She was here now with him, and he couldn't be happier.

"Are you feeling well enough to get up?" She helped him to stand when he wasn't sure that he could stand upright. But once he was up, standing on his own, he felt a good deal better. "Clyde was here too. He told me that you were dealing with the bump to your head and the magic you got from the house. The only reason that I'm up and around is because — be careful. I don't know if I could get out from under you again."

He stopped moving and stared at her. She looked up at him when he didn't move with her, and she said she was sorry. Nodding, he held onto the door jam and asked her to give him just a minute. That's all he needed. Nodding, she leaned against the doorway too.

"I have a feeling that you're not normally this talkative." She shook her head and told him she was sorry again. "No reason for that. We've only just met, and things haven't exactly been normal. I'm not either, talkative, I mean."

"I've never been one to talk to empty my head, but I'm nervous. Not just that, but unsure of myself. A feeling that I don't think I've ever had before." Brian told her that he believed that. "I don't know if you're being sarcastic or not. Are you?"

"No. I do believe that you're sure of yourself on a great many things. This, however, and me being used to magic and all that it can do, has made me feel off as well." She nodded and then looked down the hallway where they were. "Have you toured the house? Do you like it?"

"I do. It's fucking huge, however, and growing by the minute, it seems to me. So far, I've counted at least twenty bedrooms. Then when I went back to count them again, there were more. I gave up on that. I think too that the house has expanded since we arrived. According to the specs on the place, it has…had a large entrance hall that led to four other rooms as well as a staircase that led to the second floor. From there, two wings came out from the upper and lower halls to form what I can only assume were there before. Now there is an entire back wall with more bedrooms so that the house resembles a box when looking from the outside. With the inside of the square being a lovely garden." It was adjusting to their needs, he told her. "I figured as much. Then CJ, the faerie queen she told me, came by to make sure that we had everything we needed. At that time, she told me that the house would forever be adjusting to fit in with our needs until we didn't anymore. I'm not entirely sure what that means either, but I'm going with the flow right now."

"That's more than likely the best way to go." He entered the hallway and stopped to marvel at the hanging pictures that were on both sides of the hall. "Some of these are my family, along with some of yours, I'm assuming."

"I don't know who they are. They just sort of appeared when I was thinking about how in other homes like this, at least pictures of them, there were stately looking pictures of families that went down a hallway like this one." She moved closer to one of the paintings. "This one is Duke Allen Jason of Wintermount. Sound familiar?"

"Yes. That's a painting of my great-grandfather. I'll have to have my dad come over and see if he remembers any of them. Mom, too, as they could be paintings of her relatives as well." They walked down the long hallway to the staircase. "What happened to us when we were blasted? I mean, did we get any more power from the source or just his happiness in seeing us."

"I have some abilities. I guess you could call them that I'd not had before, like being able to speak to you and the rest of your family. By the way, we're having your family over for dinner tonight with mine. I'm not sure how that will go, but I think we should all meet. Or do you have other plans?" He told her that he had some things to look into but could do them at any time. "Thank you for that. I'm slightly confused. If you want the truth, how that is going to work out for them coming to eat. While my family is humans, yours aren't."

"We all eat on occasion. Not much, mind you, but we can and will enjoy a nice steak dinner." She nodded as they stepped off the last step, and she turned to him. "I've been having more meals since I've come here than I had before. It's nice, but I will tell you that it doesn't fill me up like blood will."

"Clyde gave me a book to read. I've only been glancing through it, but I think that a lot of smut books are way wrong about some of the information that they have about you guys." He laughed and took her hand into his. "Also, this might be the perfect time to tell you that I don't cook. I can, but I hate every second of it. Nothing at all to do with the kitchen area but to enjoy a meal."

"I can cook. At a few times in my long life, I did cook for larger restaurants and places that would have food service. While I do enjoy putting together a nice meal for a person or two, I'm not into feeding a horde of people." Hailey was laughing as she entered the kitchen with him. "We have a cook."

"I don't know when that happened. When I was in here earlier, there were a bunch of faeries working, but no one that was going to be cooking for us. You know, a bigger version of the little people." Mrs. Apple Pie, a faerie, introduced herself to them. Dag had hired her for the household, and she hoped that was all right. "Yes, of course."

"You know that household that you're going to be working for are vampires, correct?" She told him that she'd been a faerie here for as long as she could remember. "Then you know the house well. And it's magic."

"Oh yes, my lord. Very well. She's a bit temperamental at times, but she's a good home. Solid and full of happiness when she's wanting to be." Apple laughed. "Her name is House. Just as you'd think. I think, however, that now that the two of you are here, she'll be on her best behavior. I think she was getting bored with the lot of us around and needed a family more than anything to service."

Hailey was explaining to Apple what was going to happen for dinner tonight and gave her a count of the humans and vampires coming. Brian reached out to Clyde to thank him for the house and invited him to dinner too.

"Can't make it tonight, I'm afraid. Gracie and I have to go and see to a wizard that has been acting out. I'm still not sure of the terminology of things that she works with, but Gracie said they'd pay more attention if I were to go with her. You can understand that." He said that he did, very

much so. *"The house all right for the two of you?"*

"Perfect. I couldn't have picked a better house for us than this one." He started to ask him if he knew that the house was alive and decided that he didn't want to sound foolish. When they closed the connection, he listened to Apple and Hailey as they discussed plans for dinner. It hit him at that moment that he had a mate.

~*~

Everett couldn't get his key to work. After nearly breaking off the one that he'd been using for the last five years, he pounded on the door to get the attention of the people that had better be at the security desk. Instead of getting a person to come to the door, they spoke to him over the intercom. He hated those ridiculous things with a passion. Hated that people couldn't see his anger.

"Mr. Brown, what can I do for you?" He said that his key wasn't working. "No, it wouldn't, now would it?" He waited for more information, like they were coming to allow him in, but nothing more was said.

"Well?" The man asked him what he wanted. "I want into the offices. Christ. Do you even know who I am? I'm going to be owning this place before too much longer. Why doesn't my key work?"

"The locks have been changed. By the FBI, as a matter of fact." He asked what they wanted there. "They're here and that's all I was told. Also that I wasn't allowed to let anyone into the offices today but the Croft family. They're on their way here now, as a matter of fact."

"You'll let me in, or so help me, I'm going to fire you as soon—I'm going to fire you as soon as I get in there. Do you know who I am?" He told him who he was. "And that means that I have just as much right in there as the Crofts. Christ, this is—open this fucking door right now so that I can get into my office before the Feds do. They have no business whatsoever going through my things."

"Well, now, they seem to think differently. They've been in your office since they arrived. Some of them, anyway. The rest are going through everyone's computers too. It's kind of fun to see how quickly they can crack up a code on them and get into the workings of them." Everett asked if they'd been able to get into his computer. "Yes. They thought it was mighty nice of you to leave your password right there on your desk for them to find. Any who. I'm not going to let you in. Mr. Alex, he said that everyone is being paid for the day, so you might as well get on back to your house and—"

"I want in the fucking building right fucking now." The intercom voice said nothing more. Everett didn't know if he'd been shut off or not, but he continued to scream at the speaker for another twenty minutes. He stopped when someone spoke from behind him.

"Brown, I assume?" Everett turned quickly and nearly lost his footing. "Careful there. You don't want to be too banged up when called into the Agent's office looking over your records."

"Who the hell are you? And what the hell are you doing talking to me?" The man was well dressed, so he figured that he might be another attorney whom he'd not bothered learning his name while working here. "Are you going in? You'll have to allow me to enter with you. The stupid security team is not allowing me to enter. Also, I'm going to figure out who changed the locks without my authority."

"I changed them. And I don't need your permission to do anything to this office as it's my name on the door." He glared at Hailey when she stepped around him. "Brian, please make sure that Shithead here isn't able to enter behind me. He's going to cause enough trouble as it is, I think."

Everett watched as Hailey pulled out a key and unlocked the door. When she slipped inside of the building, he moved around the big man with her to enter too. No one was going to keep him from going into his building. Especially some neandertal looking man that seemed to be as stupid as Hailey was. However, he did move faster than he could, and the door was locked again before he could even get close enough to touch it.

"I do believe that she told you that you're not going in." Everett told the man that it was his building. "I do believe that you're wrong about that. You'll notice that I didn't call you a liar even though I'm very aware that you have lied your way into this place and done things too that would call you much more than simply a liar."

"You have no idea what you're talking about. And I will be allowed in my office, or I'll have you arrested." Everett turned just as someone pulled up in front of the building and onto the sidewalk. He wasn't sure if he was happy or disdained to see that it was several cruisers pulling in behind him and up on the sidewalk on either side of him. "See? They're here now to allow me entrance to my own building." The man only smiled at him. Then the cop spoke up from the car behind him.

He was dressed in a vest that said police on it. His gun was out like he was going to shoot him. The other officers with him were pointing their guns at him as well and hiding behind their car doors. Like that was going to save them when he wasn't even armed. Everett didn't know what was going on, but he was sure that they weren't here for him. It had to be the idiot in front of him, smiling like a lunatic.

"Mr. Brown, I'm only going to ask you this one time to step away from Mr. Tessler there. Mrs. Tessler told us to not allow you to be hurt by her husband and that she was pressing charges against you for harassing her employees." He asked the officer what he was going on about. There was no Mrs. Tessler working in this office. "That man you're there with, that's Hailey's husband. And she wants you to get away from him and her building."

"It's my fucking building. I am working hard at—what do you mean Hailey's husband? She's no more married than I am." Everett turned and looked at the man again. "You married that bitch?"

There wasn't much that he could recall about him in the hospital. When he'd woke up about ten minutes ago, all he could remember was talking to the man there and the cops being around. How did his face hurt like he'd been hit with a brick? Everett didn't have a clue. But when he'd started to access his body, seeing what else was wrong, he discovered that he had two broken ribs as well as his left leg was hurting. A nurse came into the room just as he was ready to scream for someone to come help him.

"Mr. Brown, you're not supposed to be moving around that much until we get the x-rays back." He asked her what had occurred that had brought him in here. "You called Mrs. Tessler a bitch to her lovely husband. All he did was hit you in the face, which I would have done as well, but you fell back on one of the cruisers that were there and broke your body up. Now you just lay still. You need something for pain?"

"No, I do not need anything for pain. What do you mean he hit me in the face? For calling his 'wife,' who I know isn't married, what she is?" She tsked at him and told him to hold his tongue, or he might well be suffering more pain soon. "I demand that you bring me that man here so that I can give him a piece of my mind."

"Do you have any that you can spare? 'Cause if you ask me, I'd say you don't. You're about as stupid as anyone that I've ever had in the ER before. What were you thinking when you called Hailey, a wonderful woman—a bitch right there in front of her husband? Didn't you see how big he was? Or how protective of her he is?" Shaking her head, the nurse took his blood pressure. When she was finished, she looked at him again. "You're about as dumb as two rocks, aren't you? Do you have any idea who Mr. Tessler is? Or, for that matter, who his friends are? You're barking up the wrong tree there, sir, if you think that any of them guys are going to allow you to upset or call their wives' names."

"I've been locked out of my building." An officer came into the curtained-off area before he could say much more to the nurse. She left when the officer sat down. "What are you going to do about this Tessler person hitting me? Also, I want them out of my building. It might not be in my name as yet, but it should have come to me when Old man Croft died."

"Mr. Croft was murdered. The DNA on his body is being looked at carefully. If I were you, I'd just keep my mouth shut and stop trying to claim shit that doesn't belong to you. I've seen the deed to the place. Nowhere on it does it have your name. Also, according to the will, which I've seen as well, you were not mentioned in it either. Why are you running around acting like you own that place when it's not true?"

"I want it. I'm a better attorney than any of those Crofts, and I know how to make it start seeing real money coming in. Besides, Croft told me that it was going to be mine before he died." He'd not, but that wasn't anything anyone could check up on now that the bastard was dead and out of his way. The nurse told him said if he had want in one hand in shit in the other, which did he think he was going to end up with. "I don't even have words to understand what the hell you're talking about. Of course, I'm not going to have someone shit in my hand. What a ludicrous thing to say to me. What are you, as a police officer doing about him hitting me anyway? I'm pressing charges."

"Good for you. But Mr. Brian said that he was sorry, and we believed him." He waited for her to tell him that she was joking. "He's a good man, and Mr. Dalton vouched for him. That's all we needed to know that whatever you did to provoke him, you deserved it. And if you'd of called me a bitch to my husband, he'd of not just hit you but tore you to shreds. He's a wolf."

"Oh, yes, of course, he is. And I'm the king of Canada." She told him he was no such thing as she knew what the king looked like. He was going to scream. And when he did, he was going to blame that on Hailey as well. "I want to press charges against Mr. Tessler, and because I'm paying your salary, you'll do as I tell you."

The cop sat there playing on her phone for another forty-five minutes. She never even looked up when he told her that he was going to have her arrested too. What was this fucking world coming to when a man couldn't get some kind of action with the police—

especially since he'd been wronged—to do anything for him? He'd just see about that when he was out of here.

Chapter 4

Brian stared at the two people he knew were responsible for his parents being in prison. He and Banny had been watching them for the past several hours, and they didn't make any kind of secret of what it was they were doing. Not knowing where they got the vampire book of names bothered Banny more than anything. Banny wanted to make sure they were working alone before he confronted them. And from the look of anger on his face, the two women plotting not five feet from them wouldn't be long for this world.

"What do you suppose made them think they could get away with all this?" Banny had told him earlier that he thought, though Brian wouldn't put it past her himself, that his mother had had something to do with the way vampires were being duped by them. "After dealing with my mother last month, I shouldn't be surprised to know that she was behind this. Probably making a hefty profit off it too."

Hanna Dalton, Banny's mother, had faked her death some centuries ago. Hiding the fact that she was still alive from her son and mother-in-law had worked well for the old vampire. But she lacked prestige and money. So she then decided that if she were to kill off her son, she'd be wealthy and in charge of everything. Even going as far as to kill off all older vampire so that she could make herself baby vamps and be in charge of them. With her plan, humans would have been nothing more than cattle to her. Brian was glad that she was taken care of.

Hanna had sold off Banny's father, another Bancroft, to some humans and watched while they staked him in the sun. When she'd come after Banny, her only son recently, not only did she get stripped of her magic, but she'd been killed in the process. Hanna had her hands in all sorts of plots that would be the ruination of humans that they were just finding out about.

Brian looked at his oldest friend in the world when he growled low in his throat. Then he looked to where Banny was looking. This was not going to end well for anyone. But especially for the two vamps that they'd been watching.

"Brian, rescue the child before she comes to harm. I'll stay here until I calm a bit more." Brian asked Banny if he thought that was possible. "Not really, but if I lose it now, the entire mall is going to be destroyed, and a lot of innocent people along with it."

Brian got up and made his way to the other table. Reaching out to the little girl, he figured that she was about seven. He made her think that she was his father. As soon as she came running to him, Brian picked her up in his arms and held her tightly to his body. One of the women tsked at him like he'd been wrong to mess with their playtime.

"Ah, now, that's no fun. Just leave her here, and we'll return what's left of her to you later." The compulsion was there, but he could easily ignore it. It wasn't all that hard, as they were just baby vamps. When he turned on his heel to take the child away, one of them pulled him around to face them. "Did you not hear me? I said to leave the child here so that we can have a bit of fun. Now."

Brian only smiled at them. Showing off, too, that he was a vampire while he was at it. When they backed up but didn't stop trying to get him to leave the child, he let just enough of his beast go to show them he wasn't one to fuck with. They had to be about the stupidest vampires he had ever met as they both laughed at his 'show of manliness' they called it.

Having enough of them, he raped their minds. A much easier task than he might have first thought it should have been. Their screams were cut off from the public hearing them when he saw their mouths shut as suddenly as they opened them to scream. Brian knew not only that they did indeed get the book from Hanna, but she'd come up with the plan for them to kill children of any sex so that humans would no longer produce offspring, in addition to taking vampire families to the cleaners by having them pay out large sums of money that they didn't have. Brian wondered for a moment how they thought that was going to work when they needed humans to live.

When Banny came to the table, neither of the

women seemed to understand that he was their king. Or if they did understand, then they just didn't give a shit. Yes, he thought, they were about as stupid as anyone he'd ever encountered before.

"You're breaking vampire laws. As I'm sure that you're aware of. I'm King of the vampires, all of them, and I'm here to take you to task for what you've been doing." The one that had been harassing the child told Banny to go back to his seat. Compulsion wouldn't work on Banny as he was king, but it was kind of funny to see them trying. "I'm going to have you arrested and taken to prison until such time that I can deal with you."

"What makes you think that we're going to do anything you tell us? We know who you are, king fucktard. You say you're supposed to be the king of all vampires. Well, shit noodle, we take our orders from someone else, not you. And when she's in charge, we'll see about you being king douche hole."

"You mean Hanna, my mother?" They both laughed and said that they were thrilled that they didn't have to explain to him who was going to be taking over his spot. "Hanna Dalton was brought before me for

Kathi S. Barton

breaking the very laws that I'm working to keep right with the humans. Not to mention she killed my father. She's dead. After the faeries had their fill of torturing her, she was turned to ash the moment that her magic was taken away."

"You lie." Banny turned to him and asked why it was that people assumed you were a liar when you told them something they didn't want to hear. "She's much too powerful for the likes of you to be able to just kill her off. You expect us to believe that you were able to not just kill off a powerful vampire like her but that being her son, you were able to do that as well. I call bullshit. There isn't any way someone like you is even remotely that strong and powerful."

CJ appeared before the two women. She was in all her glory too. Wings spread out, her crown, while a little askew, glowed brightly upon her head. When Donald appeared beside his mate, he too was glowing, his own crown being highlighted by the sunroofs in the mall ceiling. Christ, if he'd had the best camera in the world, it would never catch the glorious scene before him. The two women stood up and walked around CJ. They were playing with fire and seemed to not understand that.

"Are you enjoying yourself?" The women laughed and leaned closer into CJ. "I'd back off about now if I were you. I'm not in the mood to—actually, no one is ever in the mood to fuck around with idiots, but I have a lower tolerance for them than most do. I was summoned here to take care of the two of you. But first, I'm going to find out what you know."

He had already gone through their mind and was surprised by what they didn't know about the rules. But he also knew that CJ would more than likely kill them by raping not just their mind of information but she'd have her faeries going to their den and taking care of that shit as well. Whatever was there.

"You've been a bad couple of babies, haven't you? Don't answer me. I have a splitting headache, and I don't want to have to listen to you whine about things." The older of the two of them women said they didn't need to whine about anything, that she'd not harmed them. "Oh, really. What is that mess before you? Looks like your blood to me. Not to mention the little bit of brain matter that you've got up in that empty space between your ears."

Both women were bound in silver before either of them could speak. He asked Banny why he'd called CJ in, and he said that they'd killed several hundred faeries in the last few days. It was her that he was giving the first crack to the idiots. Brian could understand that. CJ was also much more powerful than Banny, anyway, because of her having both vampire and the queen's blood in her veins.

"Banny, what would you like done to these two? In the event that you didn't know, there are several more pairs just like these two doing Hanna's bidding. I can take care of all of them if you wish." Banny nodded once, his anger still so profound that he was slightly afraid of him himself. "All right, ladies. We're finished here." The ash was floating around the area where they'd been standing even as CJ and Donald disappeared.

Brian felt their deaths. Or perhaps all their deaths. It was a relief so strong that he staggered slightly from the feeling of it. Putting the child down on the floor, she didn't leave him when he'd taken the spell away for her to think of him as her dad and to return to her family. Putting his hand on her head, just too weak at the moment to read her thoughts without hurting her, he started to read her thoughts, then stopped. And he thought she'd been hurt enough today.

Brian looked at Banny when he said his name. "She's been staying in this mall for at least two weeks, more than likely longer. Her perception of time is a little off. Her parents left her here in hopes that someone would take her in. Just so long as they no longer had to deal with her. Whatever that means." Banny sat at the table with him and the girl when she sat down. "I'm going to get her something to eat. Will you keep an eye on her?"

When Banny said he would, Brian went to one of the many fast food places and ordered several different meals so that she could pick what she wanted. As he was headed back with two trays of food piled with an odd assortment of things that he had found, he noticed that the little girl and Banny were talking.

"Her name is Augustine Sheppard. She goes by Aggie." She didn't reach for the food right away. However, when Banny picked up a bag of the fries, she reached for the burger that was on the same tray. "She's been hiding out in some of the larger stores, keeping herself safe and warm. But there isn't much around here to eat for her. She's been taking cookies and other items like that that didn't require her to cook something."

"That woman over there, she runned me off yesterday." Brian looked where she was pointing and recognized the woman as one who had been giving nearly everyone in the food court trouble about cleaning up after themselves and also not eating a home-cooked meal. "She said that I was a degenerate. I know what that means. I looked it up at the bookstore when I was caught in there a couple of nights ago."

She didn't wolf down her food like he thought she would but took her time in taking small bites. When she asked for a bottle of water instead of the pop that he'd gotten, Brian touched the side of the cup and told her what it was now. Aggie stared at him for several seconds before she shrugged and took a sip of the drink.

"You're one of those magical things, aren't you?" He told her that both he and Banny were vampires. She looked out the double doors and then back at him. "We're very old. Older than almost all of the buildings around here. Some of which we had a hand in building. So we can tolerate the sun a good deal more than most. Do you know where your parents are?"

"No. I mean, I know where we were when we went on a trip. They called it a vacation, but I'm the only one that they didn't pack anything for. They got rid of my older brother this way too. He was killed, though. Somebody strangled him on account of him not putting out. I still don't know why someone would be killed over that, but I'm just a kid. Do you suppose they're going to do it to my younger brother and sister too?"

"I'd say that's a good bet. How many times have they done this to the children in your family?" Aggie told him that so far as she knew, just her and her brother. "Do you have any other relatives that you know of?"

"I have a couple of aunts, but I've no idea where they live or anything anymore. An uncle too. I don't know how they're related to me because my parents said they were only children." She ate the second burger before speaking again. "The women are Sally and Hailey. I don't know their last name. And my uncle is supposed to be someone named Alex, I think. There were grandparents too. I liked them the best. But I don't know what their names are either. Just grandma and grandpa."

Brian looked up at Banny. It just couldn't be. His mate and her family were related to this child. Reaching out to Hailey, he asked her if she could come to the mall. He didn't tell her why, but she told him that she was sort of busy at the moment filing paperwork on Brown.

"I'm sitting with a child who said that she thinks you're her aunt. She named you and Sally as such, then Alex as an uncle. Augustine is her name, but she goes by Aggie. Ring any bells?" She said that her mother was with her and she'd ask her about it. That she had a vague recollection of an Aggie but couldn't put a face to her. *"Thank you. She's been abandoned at this mall for a while now. There are other children too. I've not gotten far enough into that to see who they are yet."*

When she came back to him, Brian could feel the tension in her voice. He'd bet anything that she was gripping something tightly in her hand like she did when she was upset so she'd not lose control.

"CJ and Donald are going to pop us there. While I haven't any idea what that means, my mother and I are on our way." Brian asked if she was related to the child. *"Not biologically, but close enough."*

When she suddenly appeared in the mall, it was Olivia that stared at the little girl like she was either overwhelmed by her or terrified. He, like his mate, couldn't tell their facial expressions just yet. But when Aggie saw her, she smiled at the older woman and then started talking to her.

"Hello, grandma." Olivia nodded, her eyes filled with tears. "My parents are gone. You told me how to take care of myself if they did that to me again. And you were right."

"I'm so sorry, child. I truly am." Aggie turned back to the food, eating the Danish that he'd gotten for her to eat if nothing else tempted her. Olivia looked at him. "I was Aggie's foster mother when her parents 'lost' her once in the mall once before. No one ever believed they had lost the children any more than I did. They were arrested and charged with child neglect and sentenced to two years each for what they'd done. Aggie and her brother stayed with us for about a year after that. Then one day, the county came and picked them both up and took them back to their parents. I worried every day about what had happened to them. The police and county wouldn't tell me a single thing about them."

"Hank is dead." Aggie didn't look around when she told Olivia what had happened to her big brother. "I found me a hidey holey like you told me to do, but I didn't have a phone. But I didn't remember your number anyway. They told me that I was going to die like Hank did. That they were well and glad to be rid of me too. They're not very nice, are they?"

"Do you know how long you've been here, Aggie?" She didn't know, but Brian thought that it had to of been about a month, if not longer. "We'll have to get the police involved, you know that, don't you, honey?"

"Yes. I guess I'll be going to jail, too, huh?" It was Hailey that asked her why she thought that. "I've been stealing. I know that's not right to do, but I was starving. I even took some pretty soap and some clothes too that fit me so I'd not smell all that bad. I'd get cleaned up in the bathroom every day, so I'd not be sick. You told me that if I didn't take care that I was cleaned up every day that I'd regret it. And I did."

"You let me take care of what you might have taken for you, Aggie, all right?" Aggie looked at Hailey and smiled. "You remember me, don't you? How much fun we had while you were there."

"Yes. Your daddy would read me stories and tell me how to be effective. He told me that I could suck on the tit of society or I could make a difference. I think that I'd be the one that sucked, Aunt Hailey. Your dad, he's a really nice man. Will he be seeing to me too?" It was Olivia that told Aggie that he'd died recently. "Oh no."

Aggie took it hard that Alex Senior had died. No one mentioned that he'd been murdered. She was taking the knowledge of him no longer being there to read to her very hard already. It was Olivia that offered the child comfort by pulling her into her arms and holding her.

After talking to the few stores that Aggie had been hiding in, they found out that two of the stores had been leaving things out for the youngster. They had noticed that she was hiding and wanted to keep her safe. The other stores they'd not had any idea that anything was amiss and told him to not worry about paying them for her being around. They were all glad that Aggie was safe now. So was he.

Taking her to their home, he was glad that the faeries had anticipated her arrival. There was a room set up for the child as well as a few toys and things they thought she'd enjoy. All Aggie wanted to do after getting her belly full, and a long bath with bubbles was she wanted to sleep in her own bed. Brian didn't know what people, humans, were thinking when they simply disposed of their children like they were nothing to them.

~*~

"I'd like to be the one to adopt her." Hailey looked at her mom and didn't know what to say to her regarding adopting Aggie. "We'll stay here with you and Brian. So it won't be like she'd have to be around this old woman all the time. But she'll be happy with me, and I know that having her around will fill the emptiness in my heart since your father died…was murdered."

"I love you, Mom. You know that. But I don't think that adopting a seven-year-old is the way to get over your grief." Mom said that wasn't what she was doing. "No? Then why did you put it like that. You're wanting to adopt a little girl to fill in your heart. What about her heart? I've no problem with you adopting her. Not at all. She has always looked up to you as a mother anyway. But your reasons just don't sound like you're going to love her for the child that she is."

Mom looked angry. Her entire face with tight and pinched with it. Then, just like a snap of fingers, her mother burst into tears. It broke Hailey's heart to have done this to her, and she told her mom several times how sorry she was.

"It's not you. I wanted to blame this on you, but I swear, Hailey, this is on me. And you're so right about my reasoning behind taking her. To fill the void that your dad left in me. That's just…well, you didn't come right out and say it, but I *was* being selfish." Hailey wisely kept her mouth shut. "You're a good daughter. You always have been my favorite oldest daughter."

"Gee, thanks, Mom." They both laughed. "I don't know what is going to happen to Aggie. So far, we're only able to keep her here because of Banny. He made a few calls, and now Brian and I are okayed to foster children in situations like this. As for us adopting her? I don't know that either."

"I can understand that. The two of you have only just met, and having all of your family around would make it hard — you've not slept with him yet, have you?" She said that she'd not. "I like him. Not that it has anything to do with you sleeping with him. Though, I will tell you that I doubt very much there will be much in the way of sleeping."

"*Mother.*" Her mom laughed, and Hailey was glad for that. She'd been so sad for so long, Hailey knew. "Anyway, skipping the lack of sleep that I'll have, he's been really good to me. And he's kept his word on not pushing me into anything I'm not ready for. That's both frustrating and good for me."

"So? What do you want me to do for you, child? Tell him to push your limits and take you to bed?" She shook her head. "Then what is holding you back? Is he different than what he is out in the open? Nice out here where we can see him and mean as a rattlesnake when you're behind closed doors?"

"No. If anything, he's sweeter." She thought about what she wanted to say to her mom. They'd always had this kind of relationship. Open and honest. When her mom told her about sex and men when she was younger, Hailey knew she could go to her mom about anything. Today was no different. "I'm afraid if you want to know the truth. Not necessarily of him but what happens afterward. The magic that I've been told I'll get from being fully bonded with him. I have some now that I'm not sure how it will be useful."

"Like what sort of magic? This could be fun, I think." Hailey changed her clothing several times with her magic, and her mom was delighted with it. After asking her if she could do it too, Mom nearly fell off her chair laughing when she was able to do the same. Her outfits were the most outrageous things that she could think of. When Aggie joined them in the kitchen, she told them she had the same ability. The little girl was dressed in the most adorable pink dress that Hailey had ever seen. Mom hugged her to her. "You are beautiful no matter what you have on, but I have to admit, I'm in love with the fact that you dressed up in a dress."

After lunch, the three of them went to the store in town to find out what sort of furniture Aggie wanted for her room. Hailey knew that the faeries could do it without any trouble, but she wanted to support her local businesses as much as possible.

"I think she's overwhelmed." Hailey looked around when she heard CJ's voice in her head. *"She's afraid that she's going to be getting this stuff, and then you're going to grow tired of her and put her back in the mall. I know you won't, but that is something that she's thinking about. She's not very trustful of people right now."*

"I don't blame her. I think I would be the same way." CJ asked her if she had spoken to the child about her staying with her and Brian. *"No. I mean, I don't know what sort of plans there are for her. Sally, my sister, said that she'd take her if we didn't. I've not spoken to Brian about her, so I'm not sure what to tell my sister."*

"Do you want her as your child?" She said that she didn't know what she wanted. Then she told her that she was afraid to make promises to the little girl if there was someone else out there that wanted to take her in. *"I can understand that. But there isn't anyone. Her parents are going to be arrested this evening, and their other two children will be taken from them. So, if you decide to take her into your home as your child, then there is a good possibility*

that the other two will need a home as well. As I said, she's overwhelmed and afraid of being abandoned again."

"I would never do that to her. Or the other two. Even if Brian didn't want them, I'd leave him to raise them on my own." CJ asked if she'd spoken to Brian about Aggie. "No. I mean, we've been so busy with my dad's murder as well as Shithead that we've been talking of nothing else. You have no idea…well, you might have an idea when I say it would be nice to have one day that there wasn't something going on that needed attention right at this minute."

"Yes, I do understand that. All of us do. However, and I hate to nag at you about this, but bonding with Brian will help you in ways that you can't imagine." She told her that would take, at the very least, a miracle or something to have some alone time."

"I'll take the two of you someplace. Just say the word. I also know that the family as a whole owns a couple of islands that would be perfect for some wild and loud sex." Hailey laughed. "Yes, I had hoped that you'd laugh a bit. You're as overwhelmed as Aggie is. Talk to Brian and set up some time with him. I'm thinking he'll say tonight, and then we'll go from there. Adopt the children or not. Bonding is only going to do so much for you two. Make a decision, and I can *guarantee you that Brian will be as happy as he could be because it will make you happy."*

"Thank you." CJ said that she'd be there for her whenever she needed. *"Thank you for that as well. I think more than anything, I'm getting some good friends out of this relationship."*

Closing the connection with CJ, Hailey reached for Brian. He sounded slightly stressed, and she hated to add to it. However, when she told him what she wanted to do, she could almost taste his happiness through their link.

"That would make me a very happy person to adopt those children. I was actually going to talk to you about it tonight." She told him that she had plans for tonight. *"Oh. With your family, I'm guessing?"*

"No. With you. CJ said that she'd take us someplace where we could have loud and wild sex. Are you all right with that?" When he didn't say anything, she started to worry. *"Or not, I guess. I just thought that it — "*

"Christ, Hailey, I've been taking at the very least five cold showers a day just thinking about having you. Then you go and spring this on me, and I'm hard again. Too hard to bend over and pick up the paperwork that I dropped when

you suggested it." She laughed, and he did as well. *"No pressure, right? I mean, CJ didn't tell you to do this. She would, I think. She's very pushy."*

"No. I've been wanting to…you know, have sex with you for a week now. But I'm not very good at bringing it up. What I mean is I didn't know how. I'm not…I guess you could say that I'm not very good at starting something like this for fear of being turned down. It wouldn't be the first time just so you know." He sounded incredulous when he asked her if the person was stupid or blind. *"I'm not sure. But he did tell me that I was too bossy at work and I'd more than likely be in bed too. He said he didn't want to take orders when he fucked someone. I believe I dodged a big-time bullet with that one."*

"I'd say you're right. Christ, he actually turned you down? What is…you know what, I don't care what is wrong with him. I'm going to treat you like the queen that you are to me, and you're going to have so many releases that you're going to be begging me to stop." He laughed, and Hailey, in that moment, fell deeply and forever in love with Brian Tessler. She told him what she'd been thinking. *"Oh honey, I have loved you since you landed on the front steps of our forever home. And I love you more and more*

daily."

    She was an emotional wreck by the time she went to talk to Aggie. Mom was going to be with her when she told the little girl that not only was she and Brian going to adopt her, but they were going to find her brother and sister and do the same for them. That seemed to be just what she needed to hear. After the most wonderful hug, she'd ever had from Aggie, the child set to work on not only filling out her room but also getting things for her sister and brother as well.

Chapter 5

"We're supposed to meet the couple at five-thirty. I don't like this, Hankie. Things seem just a little off. And no matter how many times I go over the newspapers, there is no mention of anyone finding a little girl lost in there. Do you suppose she got killed off too?" Hank Mercer hated being called Hankie. Like he was some kind of tissue or something. But it did him little good to tell her that. She'd call him that twice as much if he were to mention it again. "Hankie, are you listening to me? I said —"

"I heard what you said, Lilith. Aggie hasn't been found, and you think she might have been killed. See? I heard you. However, I don't know what you expect me to do since you've done everything that could be done. Other than going to the police. I can see that now. 'Hey, we dropped our daughter off at the mall a couple of months ago. She was too old to sell off to a couple that wanted babies, so we just disposed of her. Do you happen to know where she might have gone off to?' Is that what you want me to do?" She told him not to be snarky. "What I want to know is, why do you figure that if someone doesn't answer you within five seconds of you asking them something that they're not paying attention. I don't get it. I was. I don't know what happened to her. Nor do I care. Does that satisfy your questions?"

"Well, who shit in your breakfast?" Standing up, he left her sitting in the little restaurant they'd come to for something to eat. He had wanted to try everything on the menu. Then she'd started yapping and had spoiled it for him.

They were going to have to sell off another kid before too much longer. They liked having money, and other than getting a job, this was the way it was working for them. As he sat on the bench about five blocks from where he'd left Lilith, he began his usual cruising to see if someone wasn't as attentive of their children as they should have been. He watched one woman dealing with a toddler and an infant in a stroller while she tried to order herself a coffee.

None of the children were his that they had. Not even the couple of dozen that they'd sold off were his. Hank wasn't able to father children. And luckily, Lilith wasn't able to carry them full term. If any of the children had ever been like her, he would have left her decades ago. She was off her noodle, and if she didn't take her meds daily, she would get out of hand and destroy all their hard work.

It was hard work too. Not only did they have to catch a parent off guard to get a child or two, but they also had to take care of the thing until they were able to sell it off. That made it all worth it. Newborns were high-end merchandise. Then so was any child that was from two to about four. After that, you had to practically give them away to get rid of them. He would just take them to the mall, wherever they were staying, and that would be the end of that. But Aggie, she'd been so helpful with the little ones that they'd kept her around for entirely too long.

She also was good at distracting the parents.

When she caught on with what they were doing, having her go and ask them something about the store they were in front of. The third time they used that ruse, and Lilith had walked off with the infant, it was all they could do to get away from the mother and police when Aggie started screaming that they'd taken the child. Dropping the kid in one of the trashcans as they were being chased was the only way they'd been able to get away. The next day they'd dropped Aggie off at the mall, and that was it for her.

When they'd gone to prison earlier in her life, she'd come back an entirely different child. She would watch them closely, and when they would get to someplace to drop off her or one of the other children they had, she'd refuse to get out of the car. Sometimes bringing people to them by her screaming that they were trying to kill her. It wasn't until after she was gone that they discovered that she'd been hoarding things. Money mostly but food too. Apparently, she'd been planning to run. Fat lot of good that had done her. She was gone out of their lives, and he was happy for it.

"What are you doing?" Lilith sat down next to

him, and he ignored her for watching the woman. "I asked you a question. And before you accuse me of not giving you time to answer, I counted to twenty before I asked you again."

"I'm working. One of us has to since all you want to do is sit around and spend money like we still have it. Did you know that the fifty grand that we got from the last couple two weeks ago is all but gone?" She said that they'd had fun, both of them had. "Fun or not, we don't have the funds to get gas in the car at the rate that you're spending money. Meeting this couple today is going to make or break us. I'm working on that now."

"We don't need another baby just yet. We have that one at the house." They did with a five-year-old and a six-year-old watching over him that he'd been trying to sell off for two months now. "We never take on more than one infant at a time. It's too much work."

"Work for who, Lilith? I'm the one that gets up in the middle of the night with the little fuckers. I change their diapers and feed them. You just sit around and bitch about how much noise they make. You'd think for as long as we've been doing this, you'd know that the little shits are noisy. Christ, even the older two are noisy as fuck sometimes. Always wanting to go home and shit. If we have two infants to sell off, we can take a loss on the other two to get rid of them."

"I never thought of that." It was because she didn't listen when he told her several times over the last three or four years that was what they needed to do. He asked her if she'd taken her meds today. "No. I've been feeling really good without them, and I hate the way they make me feel like I'm drugged up."

"You *are* drugged up, dumb ass. Do you want to have another issue like the last time you thought you knew more than your doctor did about your medications? I'm betting the people that live in that house now that we're gone are still finding bits of blood and bone around. Christ, the mess you made when that kid asked you for a drink of water." She said that she didn't remember that happening. She did. Lilith didn't like to admit that she'd fucked up. That was all. "Take them, Lilith, or I'm leaving you high and dry. You know that I will. I've done it before."

There were times when he wished that he'd just stayed away. Like today. When the woman turned to the child in the stroller, he decided that it wasn't going to work out and began scanning the mall for other kids. There seemed to be enough strollers around that he didn't think there was going to be a problem for him snatching a kid.

"You'll not get anyone so long as I'm around." He asked Lilith what she'd said. When she told him she wasn't speaking to him, he turned back to the women with strollers around him. *"Do you really think that this is all right? For you to snatch children literally right in front of their parent's noses? It's not in the event that you were going to say that it was all right."*

"Who is this? Where are you?" She, the voice, told him that she was nearby, but she was hidden from him. "How is that even possible. Nearby? But hidden? That is just stupid. Where are you? Show yourself."

She did. There was no walking up to him when she appeared. No warning that she was just going to be there. In a blink of an eye, his eyes, she was right there.

Christ, he nearly fell off the back of the bench when she was suddenly right fucking in front of him. And if that wasn't scary enough, she looked like she had wings. Big fucking ones that were touching the floor. Then she was gone.

"I'm the faerie queen. CJ." He told her that was a stupid name. *"Oh, and Hankie isn't? You do sound like dirty used toilet paper when she calls you that. I think that I'd change my name if I were you. Or go by your middle one. No, that won't work either. She'd find a way to shorten that too. Eddie Weddie. Or perhaps Edwardo pervo. No, that doesn't have a ring to it like Eddie Weddie does. But I'm getting off-topic here. You'll not be able to take or snatch, as you call it, any more children. They're going to be off-limits to you. In fact, if you try again, you'll be arrested. And that's what I want."*

"What the fuck are you going on about? It's not my fault that people don't watch their kids like they're supposed to. I'd not have to take them if they were watching them better. I think of it as teaching them a lesson." Lilith asked him who he was talking to. The voice, CJ, told him to just think about what he wanted to say to her, and no one would make fun of him. "She damned well better not be making fun of me." But he did as he was told and watched as Lilith wandered off.

"I'll have a word with Lilith in a little while. Neither of you is very bright, I've discovered. And it will be my

pleasure in taking the two of you down." He told her she was full of shit. *"Oh, Hankie Wankie, you are so mean to me."* Then she laughed. *"Did you know that Aggie knows all your secrets? Not only that, but she's making plans to have her — oops, I shouldn't have told you that. But that's done now. The other children at the house, the three little ones, they've been taken into a very safe home already."*

"You stole my kids?" The laughter, while pretty and reminding him of the wind chimes his mother used to have hanging on the porch when he was a child, was scaring him. Hank had no idea why, but he thought that having this person or thing as an enemy was going to cost him big time. *"What will it take for you to return them and leave me the hell alone? I have plans with those brats, and you taking them is going to cost me. And you when I find you."*

"I told you, I was here. Would you like for me to come see you again? And to be honest, Hankie Wankie, they weren't yours in the first place. You stole them first. I'm just giving them back so that they'll be in a safe and better environment than the one that you and Lilith had in mind for them." He said no, he didn't want to see her. Too quickly, too, he thought. *"All right, Hankie Wankie, I*

want you to look in the direction where the woman and the stroller was when you saw them. Go on, have a look. I'll wait on you. I have to paint my nails anyway. You go on ahead and have a look at my power."

He did. However, it took him a few moments to understand what he was seeing. Then when he realized that it was a bunch of little bugs crawling all over the front of the store, he nearly cried out. It was then that they seemed to notice that he was staring at them and came at him like a horde on the game he liked to play that had zombies in it. Standing up, he was going to run when CJ told him to sit down and shut up.

"They'll kill you with so much pain that will have you longing for death if you don't listen to what I'm telling you." He asked her how that was possible. *"Would you like a demonstration? All right."*

A dozen or so of the bugs hit him. That was all he could think about. What they'd done was hit him with their bodies. His face was in pain as well as his hands, where he'd tried to ward them off. Slapping at them with his hands made them double down on what they were doing to him. Looking at his hands when they stopped hitting him, he thought that they looked like hamburger. Like he'd been ground up and spit out of one of those roller machines that made beef steaks into hamburger.

"What did you do to me?" She told him that he'd wanted a demo, and she gave it to him. *"Demo? They fucking ruined my hands. I can't imagine what my face looks like."*

Suddenly he knew. An image of his face was right there in his mind to see the damage that had been done to him. It was worse than his hands. There were small holes all over his face and ears. Blood dripped from each little spot like he'd cut himself shaving. Touching his face, he could feel the blood as it trickled down from the wounds. Some of the wounds were so close to his eyes that he thought himself lucky in that they'd not jabbed him there.

"I didn't want them to blind you, Hankie Wankie. Just show you what they could do if you don't do as I tell you." He screamed at her to stop calling him that ridiculous name, then asked her what she wanted. *"Why I want you to turn yourself into the police. It will be better for you in the long run if you do it my way. Or not. I could give a shit what happens to you after all the heartache that you've*

caused. But you turn yourself in, and it might go easier on you."

"No." She thanked him for his time, and he felt her leave his mind. Like a rubber band snapped against his wrist, there was nothing but a void where she'd been talking to him. He didn't have any idea why, but he felt like he'd made the biggest mistake of his life just then. Nothing else would compare to him telling the supposed queen no. Hank went in search of Lilith. He could only hope that she wasn't as hurt as he'd been. Or maybe she should be. He'd not be in this shit if she'd just stopped bitching all the time about money and did what he wanted. Fucking bitch. All women were fucking bitches.

~*~

Brian didn't care for the house they were in. It had been a place that he and Hailey had been taken to when CJ said that she could help them out with a special place. However, this place looked not just run down, but it looked like it should have been closed up about a hundred years ago. He could also tell that Hailey was thinking the same thing. That they'd been somehow transported to someplace less than honeymoon-like.

"Maybe she took us to the wrong place?" He told Hailey that he didn't know. "This place could use a good cleaning. I'd do it if I wasn't so afraid that taking the dirt off the place would have it falling down on us quicker. Can you see what is going on?"

He reached out to CJ and Donald and told them what they were seeing. It was Donald that arrived at the house with them, and he looked around then back at them. He then asked them what they were seeing.

"The place is a wreck. It's falling down around us." Donald asked them to describe what they were seeing in detail. "The window over what I think is the table is busted out. The curtains, or what is left of them, are so filthy that I'm afraid to touch them."

"The place is in perfect condition. I think it's more of the fact that you don't want this to work out between you, so you're seeing fault where there is none." It was Hailey that asked Donald what he was talking about. "Are you ready to commit to each other? What I'm thinking is that one of you is not. This house and the surrounding area is a paradise. It's in the other world, our magical world. I can't see anything wrong with this house, but that one of the two of you isn't ready for some reason."

"I'm afraid." They both turned to look at Hailey when she spoke. "I know that I want this. I do with all my heart, but I'm afraid that I'll be another disappointing lay to a man. It's happened to me before. Not just the man I was telling you about but others too."

"Hailey, I love you. You'll never be a disappointment to me. In any way." Donald disappeared, and they were left alone in the house. When he looked around, Brian could see small sparks of magic. Like it was ready to change things for the better for the two of them. "Those other men, they were clueless in how to make a woman, you scream. I plan on making you scream a great deal."

"Screaming for mercy that you've taken me on?" He kissed her on her mouth. "That was very nice. But it's not enough to satisfy you, is it? What if I can't? Will you find someone else to replace me? Will you leave me alone? To be honest with you, Brian, I don't think I could stand to live without you. I've come to love you so much that the thought of life without you is too much to bear."

"Hailey, I would never leave you. Nor could

I stand to go on without you in my life. You're my everything. And more. You're the reason that my heart beats. The reason that I've not met the sun like so many others of our kind do when they're lonely. And I was. Very much so. I love you. With all that I am." She asked him if he was going to leave her if she couldn't satisfy him. "That's not even a thought in my head nor heart. I could no more be dissatisfied with you than I could for anything in this world."

Pulling her to him, he kissed her again, showing her as gently as he could how much he loved her. When she wrapped her arms around his neck and shoulders, he pulled her even closer, letting her feel how much he needed her.

When a spark of something bright caught his attention, he ended the long kiss and turned her toward it. The curtains that were hanging over the now fixed window were bright blue, shimmering in the evening sunlight like a wing on one of the many faeries that had been at their home. Asking her what she was seeing, her happiness was something that he could have lived on for the rest of his days.

"It's cleaning up. Oh Brian, kiss me again." He

did. This time giving her more of his feelings toward her. His cock was hard, and he tried not to let her feel it, but when she reached down between them, into his pants, he nearly came all over her hand when she wrapped her hand around him. "You're so large. And thick. I can't wait to feel you inside of me."

He picked her up into his arms and paused when she giggled. It was a wonderful sound. Her laughter but her giggle, like she was giddy with happiness, made him happy too. Taking her to the bedroom as the rooms around them began to take on a luster that he'd not realized was hidden from them, he was happy to see that the bedroom and bed had caught up with the magic of the rest of the house.

"This is perfect." It was too. When Brian sat her down on her feet, they both took in the beautiful room. Not only was the room perfect for them, but there was champagne and chocolates. A fresh platter of cheeses and meats. Roses of every imaginable color were all around the room. Even a few dozen of blue ones that matched Hailey's eyes. "This is all so romantic, don't you think?"

"Yes. You are." She told him that she meant the

room. "The room, for all its beauty, pales in comparison to the stunning woman that you are."

Picking her up again when she seemed to be speechless, he laid her gently on the bed. As soon as he lay beside her, the bed stretched and widened to fit his size. Taking his time undoing the buttons on her blouse, he kissed her flesh as it was uncovered. When he got to the laciness of her bra, he licked along the edges to get to her nipple. Her sigh of pleasure was all the encouragement that he needed to roll over her and between her legs.

It took him very little time to undress her. Once he had her pants undone, he moved over so that he could remove them from her legs. Leaving her panties and bra on her, a beautiful blue color that looked so tasty against her skin, he stared at the masterpiece before him, marveling that she was all his. She cupped her silk-covered breasts and asked him if he was going to make love to her.

"Yes. Forever." Using a bit of his beast, he cut the small material that was between her breasts. When her nipples caught on the material, he leaned over her and licked them through the softness. Exposing her breasts, he suckled at them over and over, taking small nips of them as he did so. When she wrapped her legs around his, it was all he could do not to take her hard and quickly. He wanted this to last. To give her as much pleasure as he could until she begged him to stop.

He made love to her with his hands and mouth. Touching her everywhere he could reach, Brian loved the way her soft sighs and loud ones made him feel. As he took off her panties, the smell of them scenting the air around him, he put them in his pocket to keep. Making his way down her body, over her ribs and belly, he licked her naval and ribs to the delight and enjoyment of Hailey. Even as he got rid of his clothing, he knew that he wasn't going to last long.

"Eat me." He couldn't have had a command he was more willing to do than that one. Licking her from gate to clit, he took his time with the swollen nubbin. When she cried out with her release, he had to work quickly in order to catch all her cream. Sliding his tongue into her, he was rewarded with the most delicious taste of his entire life.

Brian was lost in his need to drink from Hailey. When she jerked his head up from her, he could only stare at the sight before him. She was, simply put, beautiful. Her breasts had been abused slightly by her own hands. Her body was taut with need. The color of her eyes were so dark that he had trouble remembering how lovely they'd been before. They were no less beautiful now, but it was the added need of her that made them shine.

"Take me. Before I die here." He moved up her body, kissing her over and over at each place that he had to pause. When she threatened him with a stake through his heart, he laughed slightly and took both of her hands above her head and held them there. Sliding into her slowly, it was her scream, loud and long, that had him pressing forward more until he was deep inside of her. "Take me. Please. I need to feel your cum inside of me. Your cock is making me come hard. Please, Brian. Take me over the hill forever."

With her hands captured, he explored her as he took her slowly. When she cried out at each of her releases, he made sure that she was ready to come again and again by teasing her body, her skin. Releasing her hands, he felt her nails dig deeply into his back, her hands soothing the wounds by rubbing her fingers up and down his back. When he felt his body fill with the need to claim her, she bared her neck to him, and he bit down on her pounding pulse.

Dizzy with her rich blood, he drank deeply of her, careful not to hurt her. When she came again and again, he knew that he was going to release soon, and when he did, he was sure that it was going to be painful, not for her but for himself. He'd been wanting this since setting eyes on her the first time, and he was not disappointed in anything that she had to offer him. When his body tightened up, it was all he could do to hang onto his sanity as his body pounded hers with a release of his own. It was too much and, again, not enough when he came a second, then a third and fourth time deep inside of his mate.

Waking, he rolled to his side when he realized that he was more than likely crushing Hailey. She was out, her soft breaths making him aware that she was well and truly sated. As he reached below them to cover them up, Hailey told him that she was going to sleep forever and that he'd worn her out.

"I'm glad to hear that. When you're rested, I'll start again." Hailey lifted her head slightly and glared at him. Laughing and pulling her into his arms. "I don't think I could do that again if I was forced to do it. Not this quickly, however. I think if we make love like that all the time, I'm going to be testing my immortality to the limits. How about you?"

She was asleep. While she didn't snore, not at all, she was dead to the world right now. Pulling her into his body, rolling her over him so that he could hold her tightly, Brian thought of himself as the luckiest man in the world. Not only did he have the greatest mate of all time, she was someone that could match him move for move. Closing his eyes, he thought of all the things that he might well have missed had he ended his life as he'd wanted to over the decades because he'd thought never to find the love of his life like Hailey was.

Brian went to sleep thinking about life with Hailey. There was nothing that he could equate to having her in his life to anything that he might have dreamed of when he'd been thinking of a mate. Their life would never be boring or normal, and he found that he just didn't care so long as she was by his side.

Chapter 6

"Mr. Brown, do you know why you're here today? Because if you were to ask me, I'd say that you do not, sir. I don't know what you're going on about that the Croft family firm is yours, but I'm here to set that record straight for you today so that we can get going on the trial for other things that have come to light in recent days. Mr. Brown, you are not now, nor have you ever been the cwner or in with a partnership with Croft and Croft Law Firm. I have been made aware that you were, at one time, ten years ago, as a matter of fact, *asked* to enter into a partnership with the firm. However, you have never been able to get the funds needed to join. Is that about right?" Everett said that he had the money now as soon as Hailey Croft left the firm to him, as he was supposed to have it when Mr. Croft died. "That isn't true either. You were never mentioned in the will of Mr. Croft Senior. It's a safe bet, since you weren't named in the will, that you were not given the firm once he had passed. His daughter Hailey and her brother Alex have been given the firm. Again, there was no mention of you taking it from the Croft family. I'd like for you to get that notion out of your head right now. You're becoming tedious constantly trying to say that you own something that you do not."

"I should be the rightful owner. You've no idea how hard I have worked to make it my business. This woman, that one there, she is forever at the office, and I cannot get anything done watching what she is doing all the time." Shithead pointed to her, and Hailey blew him kisses. "See? Right there is the reason that her father left the firm to me. She's childish and immature. I demand that you make her sign it over to me this instant."

"No, I'm not going to do that, Mr. Brown. But I will tell you what I'm going to do. I'm going to go ahead with this pretrial thing…unless you want to plead out on it now. That sure would make me happy." Shithead asked why they were having a pretrial, then changed his mind and said for the judge to go ahead. "Are you saying that you wish to go ahead with the sentencing part of this, or do you want to go ahead and have a trial? Either is all right with me. But the first one would make things a good deal—"

"Not that I care how easy or not things are for you. I want this over with. The sentencing part. Go ahead." Brown looked at her and then back at the judge. "You put on as many years as you can with this. It will make me a happy man too."

"All right then. Just give me a minute here to see what I have to work with. You're sure you want as many years on this sentence as I can make? That seems like—"

"Yes, yes. Get it over with. I need things to get done today, and I'm not getting anything done having you ask me every ten seconds what I'm sure about. I'm sure. As sure as I'm standing here." The judge glanced at her and then shrugged. "Good lord, you'd think that you'd never had a sentencing hearing before."

Hailey had a feeling that things were not going as Shithead thought they would. First of all, she was about as sure as she could be that Shithead thought that she was the one that was being sentenced. Also and this one made her laugh to herself a great deal that he also thought that he was going to be walking away with the Croft Firm in his hands to do with as he pleased.

With the help of the Dalton Kiss, she'd not only gotten all the locks changed on several of the buildings that they owned downtown, including the firm. But she'd been able to have her father exhumed, and his death had been ruled as a murder. Shithead had left enough prints and DNA on her Dad's body that it was hard to find an equal amount on her dad that had been left behind.

The coroner, who had done the original autopsy, had been arrested for his part in the coverup. Not only had he botched the entire thing up and falsified her dad's death certificate, but he'd also left the gun that had killed him inside the coffin as well. The funeral home, also liable for the way things were handled, was closed down, and their records were being gone over by the FEDs even as they sat here. There were going to be a lot of high-office people being unemployed by the end of the day.

"All right, Mr. Brown, I have it all here. How would you like this? All at once, or do you want me to draw it out and tell you how much sentencing I've come up with for each of the crimes committed. Since you've been so cooperative about this, I don't even mind if you go the whole route." Smiling like a loon, Shithead turned to her and told the judge to just give him the final total. "All right. I'm sentencing you, Everett Brown Jr., to seven life terms without parole. These will run concurrently with the other sentences that you have with the state of —"

"What did you just say?" Shithead looked about as shocked as Hailey had ever seen him. "You mean Hailey Croft. I think she's supposed to be married, but I have no idea. You meant that she was the one being sentenced. Right?"

"No. I told you several times, as a matter of fact, that you were on trial, and when I asked you if you needed an attorney, you declined and said you'd represent yourself. Also, and this might come as a huge surprise to you, Hailey Croft Tessler is a model resident of this area. She has a good job and a nice husband. I have absolutely no idea why you thought that she'd be in trouble, but you were warned that this was all on you." Shithead said that he'd made a mistake. "I do hope that you mean you've made a mistake. Because I did exactly what you asked of me. After numerous times being told that this was a pretrial for you."

"No. No, you see, I thought this was for her. You have to sentence her." The judge did not look amused and asked Shithead if he understood the seating arrangements that he was currently in. "I just thought things were different for someone such as myself. You know, I get to sit up here alone so that I could have the spotlight on myself. I had—you've messed up. Now, sentence Hailey so that I can take over the firm that belongs to me."

"When will you get it in your head that the firm does not belong to you, young man? It is the Croft law firm. Not Croft and Brown. Not Brown. It is Croft. Now. As I said, you have been sentenced for the crimes that you committed. I have no doubt you put yourself in the position of thinking you are the rightful owner of the firm. However, killing Mr. Croft, a good man, to gain the access you so desperately wanted and trying to kill off his son and daughter is not the way to go about it. You are hereby remanded over to the FBI, where they will have their own trial about how you've been stealing from said firm as well as sending false billing through the mail system. If you were to ask me, young man, I'd say you should have been a good deal smarter than you were for being an attorney."

The banging of the gavel was starkly loud to the quiet of the room. Anger was there too. Not just from the judge but Shithead as well. When he was taken into custody and dragged away, no one in the courtroom moved or spoke. Either from shock or just wondering what was going to come next, they didn't even get up to leave then the judge called an hour for lunch.

"The families have arrived." Nodding, she looked down at Aggie. She'd been with them all morning and was looking a little lost. Brian got down to her level when he could see too that she was upset. "You want them to go to their homes, don't you? I mean, we're still looking for your parents, honey."

Once the children from the house and some of the things they'd found in the home of Hank and Lilith Mercer had been tested for DNA, they discovered that none of the children had been the Mercers. Not only that, but they had kept things that had belonged to the other children that they'd taken and sold off in plastic storage bags, with not just their names on the bags but also where they had taken them from as well as the date and time. There was also a small notebook with each child's personal things that said who the Mercers sold them to as well as how much.

It was easy to trace where the children had come from and for them to try and get them back to their parents. The three at the home that day were meeting with their parents or relatives. Also, the two other children that had been chained up in the garage too were going to find their parents as well. Aggie, she was the odd child out in that they'd found nothing about her in the house. Not even a notebook where they'd tried to sell her off.

"I do, but I'm going to miss them so much." All the kids had been examined in the hospital, including Aggie. They were cleaned up now, fed and looking a good deal better than they had a week ago. Now all they had to do was have the Mercers arrested so that there would be some sense of safety around the state.

"They'll be happy too, don't you think?"

"I do." The room they were meeting in was large. The local restaurant had invited them to have the gathering at their private dining area, and tiny food was being served. It wasn't really tiny, but that was what Aggie had called it when she'd seen it. Tiny food for children.

Introductions were made with the parents to the children. Like Aggie had, some of the children had been away from their parents for a long time. In a child's life, Hailey knew, they changed so quickly that, at times, it was hard to keep up with them, like Banny and Kelly's daughters. It seemed to her that they changed by the hour.

The infant that had been for sale was recognized first. Of course, he'd only been away from his parents for a few days, but it was enough that the parents had given up hope of ever seeing him again. Thomas, too, went right to his parents as soon as they entered the room. It took them no time at all to be sobbing like the first couple about how they never thought of seeing him again.

The other two children, away from their parents

for over three months each, had been welcomed too by their parents. Hailey noticed that the mothers never let go of their little ones, and she was happy to see that. Not that this was their fault that they'd been taken, but she'd bet anything that they'd be watched over hard until they left home. Perhaps even after that.

Aggie watched the children being reunited with their families. It was Peter, her best friend, that came to get her and take her to meet his parents. The two of them had been taken around the same time, Peter had told them, and they had been there for each other since. Mrs. Carter, Peter's mother, hugged Aggie too. Telling her how thankful she was for saving her son for her.

Letting the children talk, she and Brian sat down with the Carters and told them what they'd been able to find out. They were still looking for the couple who had taken the children. It was Brian that explained they were waiting to catch them in the act of another kidnapping. That way, their sentencing would stick better in a court of law.

"But the parents. Oh my, I know how that feels to lose your child. I don't know if I'd be able to —"

"I'm sorry. I should explain. My sister-in-law, who is an FBI agent, is going to pose as the mother of twins. She has a set of little girls of her own, but they're using dolls for this kidnapping. That way, no one is hurt." Mrs. Carter looked so relieved that she felt horrible for telling her about it. But she assured her that so long as they were getting those monsters off the streets, she was fine with how they were handling it. She turned to look at Peter and Aggie, who were sharing a plate of vegetables with each other.

"They're so close. Peter, that's all he could talk about was how she had saved him so many times while they were gone. That she'd even taken a beating for him." She looked at them. "When you called us and let us speak to Peter, he asked us to adopt Aggie, or she'd be put into the system. I have since found out that you two were going to take her."

Hailey looked at Brian before turning and speaking to the Carters. "I — We both think that they'll both be better off with each other. We love all the children, but having her happy is all we really wanted. While she was staying with us and the other children until the DNA tests came back, they renewed their bond and protected each other from everything. Not that we ever did anything to warrant them being protective, but we do think that they'd be better off together. Also, we'd like to ensure that all your children have their needs met. We've set up a trust fund for them all to go to a college of their choosing as well as a bit of money coming to your family each month to help with any medical needs, including seeing someone about any trauma they might have to deal with."

"I don't know what to say." Hailey said for them to just say thank you. "Yes, thank you very much. We weren't expecting this. To be honest, it was going to be difficult for us to do this, but we wanted it for our son. Oh, Mr. and Mrs. Tessler, you've no idea how…well, I can't thank you enough. Neither of us can. Thank you."

After the paperwork was taken care of, the little families left to go to their homes. Now all they had to do was take care of the Mercers so that they spent a good long time in jail. Hailey would be happy if it was the rest of their lives. And that was what she was going to fight for when she took them to trial. Hopefully, very soon.

~*~

"You do know that these dolls are the worst looking things I've ever seen. I wouldn't put it past them to walk away when they see how ugly they are. I'm tweaking them." Brian laughed when Kelly leaned over to the two dolls in her carriage and did just that. He was pretending to be her husband, as Banny had flipped out when it was suggested that Kelly be alone with the 'twins.' *"How is Banny doing? I do hope he chills out soon. Doesn't he get that I'm immortal like he is?"* Hailey laughed when she answered Kelly.

"I don't think he cares right now. But he's holding your daughters and telling them if you so much as break a nail, an old platitude, he was going to test all of our immortality. I don't know why he skips right over just telling me not to let you get hurt and goes right for my death, but there you go." He heard from CJ that the Mercers were on their way to the mall. "I'm so glad that CJ nudged them to go out looking for babies today. The waiting on them was driving me over the edge. I know it was everyone else as well."

Brian watched the couple and decided that they'd been messing with the faeries again before the little ones were called away. Both of them looked worse for wear, and he was happy about that. When they sat in their usual spot in the food court to watch the parents, he decided that it was time for him to walk into the store they were in front of. He hated leaving Kelly on her own, but the plan they had called for him to leave her so that she'd be picked up on the Mercer's radar.

"Hank is moving now. It looks to me that Lilith is looking at another couple. I know from what CJ told us about reading their mind that Hank wants more than one child to sell off this time, as it's getting harder for them to do anything. Do you suppose it's because they don't have any children to fall back on? It seems to me that they would have quit when they lost the kids they'd already kidnapped." Brian told Hailey that he thought they were beyond stupid and was doing what they could to get what they needed and damn what everyone else thinks. "There is that. All right. Lilith is moving toward Hank. Stay in the store for now, Brian."

He said that he was standing next to Kelly with his magic hiding him from everyone else. She told him that was an excellent idea.

"I have them on occasion." They both laughed, and it helped loosen the tension that he was feeling.

When Lilith struck up a conversation with Kelly, she turned her back to the stroller. Hank took the stroller and moved away to the next store. As soon as Lilith joined him, they were finished. "She's asking her about the dress in the window. I guess she doesn't have much in the way of tastes, either. The dress is obviously for someone about a quarter of her age. As soon as she's gone, I'll stay with Kelly."

"Yes, all right." When Lilith walked away, Brian came out of the store. It was what was planned. Just as Kelly 'noticed' that her children were missing, and started screaming that her babies were missing. The Feds caught the Mercers loading the dolls into their car. He didn't know how well Kelly had tweaked the dolls, but it must have fooled the two of them. They were clueless that they'd just kidnapped a couple of cheap dollies that Kelly had picked up on the way into the mall.

Kelly had a backup for this plan all the way up to the president. He was glad that she'd been able to have a plan worked out that would get the two kidnappers arrested. Not only for kidnapping but the death of three of the children that they had taken too. When all was

Kathi S. Barton

said and done, the two of them would be spending the rest of their lives in prison. However, he didn't think they'd last all that long. People had a tendency to not live all that long when accused of harming children. Brian hoped that they suffered too, like the parents of the children that had been taken by them.

"How about some dinner, just the two of us?" He told Hailey that was an excellent idea. "Yes, well, I have them on occasion as well. You pick, and we'll have a wonderful time."

"I love that." He looked around the mall and then back at her. "We do need a few things. Did you want to get them here? Like sheets for the spare bedrooms. Now that the ones that kids were staying in are empty, we should decorate them suitable for someone coming to visit."

"Great." They headed toward one of the anchor stores to do some shopping. Hailey turned to him with the saddest look on her face. "I'm going to miss having the children all around. I know you will as well. I'm looking forward to your sister coming to visit tomorrow with her kids."

So was he. He loved his family and missed them

a great deal when apart. The house was making room for all of them by making suites for the families to stay in while visiting. His brother Peter was going to take the castle as Brian decided that he'd rather not live in it full time. With that, he was going to open his home for Christmas as they had done every year since he'd been a child and celebrate the holiday there.

By the time their reservations were nearly ready, they'd made three trips to the car with things they'd gotten for their house. Tomorrow there was going to be a delivery of things that they couldn't stuff into the car. Brian thought they'd done a wonderful job tonight, and he was looking forward to a nice relaxing dinner with his mate.

Dinner was wonderful. He was sure that the company had been the reason for it for the most part. They had eaten well, and he was full as he'd ever been with having a meal. As they were walking out to their car, he wondered what the next few decades would bring for the two of them. He knew it was going to be more than he could have imagined.

"I've decided to sell my half of the firm to my brother." He said that was fine with him if that was what she wanted. "I do. Not that I'd take any money for it, but I do want Alex to be able to work the way that he wants. I was, and still am, too pushy when it comes to getting the work done. I can see that now. And if I want to have any kind of life with you — which I really do, then I'm going to have to give up on being an attorney. It's something that I really enjoyed for a time. Mostly because I was able to work with my dad. But now that he's gone, it has sort of lost its luster for me."

"I can understand that. It's sort of like the castle that I'm going to turn over to my brother. It was wonderful to be able to go there and stay with my parents and family around, but since they've decided that they want to live in a house that is more suited to them, the castle would only be something that I'd open during the holidays. With my brother living there, I think he'll have it a happy place again. Not a place where my parents assumed they'd die in." She told him that sounded harsh. "I didn't mean that the way that it sounded."

"It's all right. I knew what you meant." They were driving home, nearly there, when she spoke again. "I know that we've not talked about it too much, but I'd really like to have children with you. Kelly said that there was about a fifty-fifty chance of me having children with you. She seems to think that the reason that she was able to conceive is because she has vampire in her bloodline. I don't care. It's fun trying."

"Yes, it is at that." They'd been making love every day since the first time. Not only did they make love in the house but outside, in the garage as well as the car. The latter of the places had taken a hard beating from them, but it had been so much fun. "Finding new places has been the best time of my life, I have to admit."

Once they were home, the faeries emptied the car for them. They knew that it was important to support local businesses, so they weren't upset when they knew that they could have made all the things that they'd purchased. It was sort of fun for the two of them to watch them explore the new additions to the house to see how they were put together. Mostly they were disappointed in the quality of the items and were upgrading them even as they were arranging them around the house.

After Hailey went up to bed, he needed little

sleep since he was older. He sat at his computer to have a look at their finances. They were in really good shape, thanks mostly to Hailey's income, but they didn't have a great deal of money like he wished they had. Just as he was thinking that he needed to find a way to add to their coffers, Banny called him. It was always a shock to him when he used a phone. Banny was so old world that he was surprised that he even knew how to use a computer.

"I have a proposition for you." He said that he'd do anything that he needed, then related what he'd been thinking about. "Good, this is going to fit right in with your thoughts. I need someone to keep an eye on some of the things going on in town. Nothing bad, mind you, but just having someone to have a look around at some of the things that might need to be done. I grew up here, so I think I might well be blinded by that. Like sidewalks. I just found out today that there isn't anyone fixing them because they'd not been fixed for a lot of years, and people just assumed that they were never going to be fixed."

"I can do that for you, but I don't know what that has to do with me finding a way to put more money in the bank for us. I mean, I could do that by just talking a walk around with Hailey. I love showing her off." Banny laughed. "What are you really hoping that I'll do for you. Like I said, I'd do anything for you."

"I need for you to head up a crew or crews that would be at your disposal in getting things fixed up as soon as they're found. It was also pointed out to me that there are a few buildings that need to be either torn down or renovated. I'm thinking that a couple of them are well past the renovating point." Brian told him that he'd love to do that for him. "Good. I'm not going to give you a budget to work with. I know how things can run over and not be what you thought when you started out. Also, I'm going to pay you a very good wage for taking this off my back for me. You've no idea, well perhaps you do, how much work I have going right now. I'm having too much fun with my daughters to care very much about the town at the moment. I'm sure that will change when they get older, like in their hundreds, but for now, I don't want to miss a single thing about their lives. It's heady being a dad to twins."

"I know what you're saying. Even though they

weren't our children, it was so much fun making sure they were doing all right. They weren't even our kids, and we were terrified of doing something wrong." They both laughed. "All right. I'll do it. It might be just what I need to get myself some savings."

"Great. Also, you should know that the government is giving a reward to you and Hailey for your part in the apprehension of the Mercers. Kelly told them to give the money to the two of you as she is quite happy to have been a part of the planning. I hope that doesn't piss either of you off." He told his dearest friend what they'd spent tonight and how much it had left in his checking account. "You dumbass, why didn't you say you were leaning close to being broke. You know...fuck it. I'm going to put some money in your account. And if I hear one word about how we shouldn't have done it, I'll tell Kelly to take you to task. You know she won't hold back in putting you in your place."

"Yes, threatening me with your wife is a smart move. What if I tell her what you said?" Banny told him that she would march right over to him and put him into place right now. "I've no doubt that she would too. All right. What else did you call me for? I know you well enough that you do have something else to talk about. Spill it."

"I want you to help me with a couple of other projects too. I want you to run for Mayor." It was on the tip of his tongue to tell Banny he had no desire to be anything remotely like that when Banny continued. "The town needs someone in office that isn't going to be taking from the allowances of the school board and using it for their own personal use. Kelly just happened to find out today that our current mayor is doing that. He's also using school funding to fund his own personal trips. He has a jet in his name, sitting in the airport now. I hadn't any idea that there was that much money in the school funding. But I want him out of there. And other than draining him, like she wanted to do, Kelly agreed with me in telling you to take the job."

"Actually, I think that Hailey would be better suited to the mayor job than me." Banny was quiet for a couple of minutes, then told him he thought that would work better. "She's looking for something to do now, and with her having a law degree, she'd be great at it. I'll talk to her in the morning about it."

"That's perfect. I can't wait to tell Kelly. Of course, I'm going to tell her that it was my idea, just so you know." They were both laughing as they got off the phone. Brian could see his Hailey kicking ass as mayor. She'd get things done too. He was looking forward to telling her and that it had been his idea all along.

Chapter 7

Years later

Hailey was happy to see that she was going to be the mayor again. It was her third term but with ten years between her first and second time to this one. She had been begged by no less than fifty people for her to run again because nothing was being done by the current mayor. Sitting in her office at home, she fielded calls congratulating her for an hour before she got up and went outside to find Brian. He'd been working in their garden, a place he told her that made him happy since they'd had breakfast this morning. Well, she'd had it. He watched her eat.

"I just got word that I won the seat." He picked

her up and swung her around to show how happy he was for her. "Thank you. How are things going on out here for you?"

"I have carrots. I never knew how different they could taste from the ones in the store. They're actually much better here in my little plot." Little? The garden was monstrous, and when he was finished with it, several families, if not all of them, would benefit from him being bored in the summer months. "Also, one of my pepper plants is doing so well, I might have enough to make a big salad."

"You'll have more than enough to make a hundred salads, and we both know it. With the help of the queen of all things and the few thousand faeries running around, there is no way for you to fail at being a farmer." He laughed and then kissed her. "I'm reminding you again about the wedding this weekend. Don't think about trying to miss it."

"Never. Not this one. Aggie and Peter make a wonderful couple, and I cannot wait to see them married. I never would have thought that they'd be so well suited for each other. I'm over the moon happy for them." She told him that she was as well. "I know that the Carters are happy. Every time I speak to Donald, he tells me how happy he is."

As the children had grown up, their love for each other seemed to surpass anything that anyone had seen before. Both of them were young, only eighteen and nineteen. They'd been taking care of each other since they had been kidnapped long ago. Hailey was so happy that they'd given up custody of Aggie to the Carters all that time ago so that the kids could have a solid relationship.

"Alex is coming over later to talk to me about a couple of cases that he's working on. I think he's going to tell me that he's ready to expand again. I don't know why he feels that he has to clear it through me, but I'm glad to be able to see him." Brian pointed out to her that they only lived about three miles away. "I know, but when he comes over to the house, I get to see him all by myself. His wife is staying home with the kids. I love her too, but seeing Alex shine is so much better when I can tease him about it."

"I know what you mean. When Shawn found his mate last year, I enjoyed that more than I think he did. He was glowing with happiness. So much so that I had to tease him by wearing sunglasses around him all the time. It's fun to be able to have fun at his expense." When Brian said he was finished for the day, they went into the house. The house was still fussy at times about how it thought that it should be treated, but they'd gotten used to his antics and, for the most part, were rarely surprised anymore. However, when they walked into the house, both of them stopped just inside the doorway.

"It's summer, you know that, don't you?" There was a large real Christmas tree in the corner of the room. Under it were what looked like a thousand presents, all wrapped up in the most wonderful wrapping. "What are you doing, Mr. House?"

"It makes me feel good when I'm pretty. And I like the way the pine smells so good." She couldn't fault him for that. The house had been given the magic to talk to them about the time she'd run for mayor the first time. She and he had had a lot of fun talking things out together. "I shall take it down if it bothers you, my lady."

"It doesn't. Just don't have it around when we have company. People already think that we're loony at times. All right?" For his answer, the lights on the tree shown brighter, and the colors danced around the room at dizzying speeds. "Thank you for that. You've brightened my day as well."

She had some dinner while Brian worked on setting up some construction jobs with his company. Banny had sold the construction company to him four years ago, and the two of them were forever looking for a new project to start on. They were also about as wealthy as Banny and Kelly were because they'd been investing well since he started getting paid.

They'd not had any children as yet. She wasn't sure that it was going to happen for them. It was told to her that she should have conceived when they'd had sex at the castle. Now they were just taking in children of all kinds to keep safe while the parents were sent away or had other things going on that their children had been taken from them. Mary was one of the children that had been left behind when her parents had gone to prison. She'd been with them for five years now.

Mary would be turning eighteen next month. She knew that she didn't have to leave them just because she'd hit a milestone birthday, but she wanted to go to college in England. There were two colleges there where she wanted to pursue a law degree. Whatever she wanted, they would help her get it. She was the daughter that they'd not had. Mary was sitting in her office when Hailey entered.

"I'm almost finished here. My computer is getting an update, and I need to answer these questions before tomorrow." Hailey told her that she was only going to watch some videos and for her not to worry about it. "I have some things that I'd like to talk to you about anyway. I have an idea that when I leave here, you and Dad are going to be couch patties, as grandda calls them."

She, like the rest of the children that had come to their family, called all the elder Kiss members grandda and grandma. They loved them as much as she thought that the kids loved them. Even Banny was called grandda at times when he got a little huffy about things. That was her favorite part. His being huffy.

"We're actually planning to take a cruise soon. I think that the one that Brian chose for us is leaving a week after you do. So we'll not be patties for long." Mary asked her if the two of them would go to London with her to help her settle in. "We could do that. I think that would be more fun than being worried about how you're managing with college. You're still going to be living in the home that we own there, right?"

"Oh yeah. I love the fact that I'll have someone there for me when I get home from school. And the faeries that are going with me are about as excited as I am for this chapter in my life." She said she was as well but had to turn away when her eyes filled with tears. "Hailey, please don't cry. You'll have me crying, too, if you do that."

The two of them talked about all the things that she was going to take with her. And things that she was going to leave behind. Things that she wanted to be able to come home to when she was on a break from school. Of course, the house, like all the homes that they now owned, was filled with faeries, so there was little need for her to take things that she wanted when they could easily make it for her.

Mary went out with friends later, saying that she'd be home before too long. Saying goodbye to her friends was difficult for the teenager as she had been so outgoing that she had a great many of them. After she left, Hailey had herself a good cry. She was going to miss the younger woman.

She and Brian talked about going to London with Mary. He, like her, thought it would be much more fun for them to be there instead of going on a cruise and missing her. Not that she thought leaving her there was going to be any better. However, they'd know that she had everything that she needed before they left her.

At two in the morning, they got a call about three children that needed a safe haven. Telling the faeries to be ready for them, she and Brian, as well as Mary, went to get them at the police station. First thing that they knew they'd have to do was take them to the emergency room. Brian was an attending doctor and helped when they needed him, so it was easy for them to get all the tests they needed to take care of the children.

"Hailey?" She cautioned Mary from saying too much in front of the three and five-year-old both little girls. "They're beautiful, aren't they?"

They were a mess. Whatever had happened to have them in their care, there had been a lot of bloodshed. The younger of the two of them, Sara, had a lot of bruising on her tiny body. Some of them looked like finger marks. Like someone had grabbed her too hard, and she'd been hurt. The older girl, Hanna, was hurt too, but she was the bolder of the two of them and told them that their mommy had hurt them.

"She's a mean old bitch." Mary started to laugh but caught herself. "Well, she is. She and that person that is staying with us hurt Sara bad when she wouldn't go to sleep when they told her. It wasn't even dark out yet. I had to call the police when the mister decided that he was gonna plug her one in the head. Dirty bastards."

Hailey was both delighted and horrified by what they were being told. Hanna kept telling people to have a look at Sara first as she was littler and her body was tiny. The two little girls were going to have to stay the night, and Hailey made sure that the two of them were in the same room, one big enough that the three of them could stay with them.

It was nearly four in the morning when she was able to get the two of them settled down. Sara went to sleep right away after having a light meal of yogurt and milk. Hanna watched over her sister like she was worried about her getting hurt again. No amount of reassuring her would make her understand that they'd never harm either of them.

At about six, just as she was dozing off, she heard Mary talking to Hanna. She was telling her about how she was going to another country and that she'd be learning cyber law while away.

"I have my room all set up at the house. If you and your sister want to play with anything in there, you go right ahead. You remember me telling you about the faeries." Hanna told her that she wasn't addled. "No, of course, you're not. But I want you to be aware of them. They're there to help you get what you need. Whatever it is, so long that it's within reason."

"All I want is to have a real bed for Sara and me. And food when we want it. The rest is what my granny used to call dressing." Mary asked her where she was. "Under the porch. Momma killed her when she wouldn't turn over her check. I don't know how much money it was for, but it surely wasn't worth my granny being dumped under the porch. Someday I'm going to tell on her and get us someplace where we can get a nice good night's sleep without guns going off."

Hailey's heart broke. Looking over at Brian, she knew that he'd heard the little girl too. As she told Mary some other things that had been going on with their lives since they'd been born, she asked him if these were the children that they'd been waiting on forever."

"I think you might be right. I can feel it." They'd never adopted a child that came into their care before. It never felt right. Most of the children, with the exception of Mary, had gone to other relatives within a few months of staying with them. But almost as soon as she asked Brian, she could feel the rightness of it. That these little girls would be theirs forever.

By the time the breakfast trays were being brought around, with Mary putting her two cents in about adopting the little girls, they were contacting Kelly and Banny to see if there were others around that would take the girls. So far, she'd come up with nothing now that she knew that the grandma had been murdered. She was also going to take care that she was found as well.

When they were ready to go, being cleared by another doctor, they took them home to show them the rooms that had been set up for them. Mary took charge of the little girls, helping them with their baths and showing them how to pick out their clothing. As much as she wanted to do this by herself, she knew that the girls would relate better with Mary, so Hailey waited her turn. When they came downstairs after about an hour, Hailey was having a hard time not sobbing about how beautiful they looked in their little pink dresses and sandals. Brian decided that they'd go out tonight to have pizza. He told them all he was looking forward to having four of the best-looking women with him. Sara clapped, and Hanna just eyed him.

Dinner was a success. As they were finishing up with the food, Gracie came by to see them with Clyde. She sat down across from them and looked at them both in the eyes before she spoke.

"The police have found your granny and another body under the porch. Do you know who that is?" Sara said Daddy and Hanna explained that he had been married to their momma when they'd been born. "That's what the police thought as well. But I told them that I'd ask you. Also, I want you to know that the man that hurt you both he's dead. You know that he was shot by your momma before you called the police.

Correct?"

"I shot him." CJ nodded as if she knew that Hanna was going to say that. "He was gonna kill Sara, and I didn't want him to do that. So I found the old gun that was in my momma's room and used it on him. I would have used it on momma, too, because she was powerful upset that I'd killed him. His name was Davy something. I never called him dad like he told us to do."

"Good for you. You're both very brave. I'm very proud of you, and I'm sure that Hailey and Brian are, as well as Mary. You saved your sisters life, and that was wonderful of you." Hanna looked at CJ with a cocked brown. "You can ask any of us what you want, and we'll answer you truthfully. I want you to keep that in mind when you decide that you need to know something. All right?"

"You're a shifter thing, aren't you? All of you." CJ told Hanna that she was actually a wizard and showed her a bit of her magic. Hailey wondered what the girls would say when they found out that they were, for the most part, vampires. "My momma, she told me once that they were all fake. That I'd never seen one before.

But me and Sara we were in trouble once and had to stay in the dog house. A wolf came by and gave us some blankets to hide in the thing so we'd not catch our death. From then on, when we were in trouble again, someone would bring us food and water with some blankets. We seen a vampire once, too, didn't we, Sara?"

"Yes. He was super nice too. He gave me a drink of his blood so I'd not die. He's standing right over there." When they all turned to look, they were surprised to see Harland, Banny's father standing there. "He bringed us food, too, and helped with the sores that we had. One of mine was infected so bad that I nearly lost my leg, huh, Mr. Harland?"

"That's right." The table enlarged itself with a little help from CJ. Harland told them how he'd been out walking and discovered the children in the dog house. "If I'd had a little bit more rest by then, I'd of made sure that they were safe all the time from those people. But I was called home when my mate went into labor. I clean forgot about them after that."

Harland had three children now, not counting Banny. He'd been hard-pressed to return to the dead when CJ had first brought him back. But now he was just like the other men in the kiss, happy and thrilled to be having the time of his life with his new and wonderful family.

Making their way home, both girls peppered them with questions, and she was happy that they didn't seem to be afraid of the people around them. When she asked Brian if Hanna would be in trouble for killing Davy, he said that it was taken care of. She didn't care. So long as they were all safe and sound.

~*~

Mary helped the girls decorate their room. She remembered when she'd been able to do things to the room she'd had now and knew how overwhelming it could be for someone. But they took to the magic that they had very well, and soon they had their room — they insisted on sharing one — just the way the two of them wanted it. Mary thought they'd done a good job too.

"What's going to happen to us when someone comes to take me to jail? Will you be watching over my sister for me?" Sara was still taking naps, and Mary was happy that Hanna had waited until she was asleep before asking her questions. "I don't want to go to jail, but I didn't want to be without a sister either."

"You remember meeting Uncle Banny and Aunt Kelly?" She said that he was a funny man. "Yes, he is. But he's one of the best people around. All of them are. But Kelly took care that no one would come after the two of you."

The relief on her face was palatable. She was so glad to hear that that Hanna laid back on the bed and cried. It was the first bit of emotion that the child had shown since she'd been with them. Hugging her tightly in her arms, she told her how much she loved having her as a sister and that she was so happy that they'd been able to take care of this for her.

"My momma kept screaming at me that I was going to go to the electric chair for doing that. She said that they'd put me in a tub of water so that I'd be dead the first switch they turned on. I would have done it, gone to the chair without crying, but I'm so glad that I don't have to. I was terrified that I'd be leaving Sara alone with Momma. She didn't like either of us, but we padded her food card, she told us."

The child was much too jaded for her age. Mary

knew that she had been too when she had come to be with Hailey and Brian, but this child and her sister were street-smart and knew just how to cut through the bullshit to get to the truth. After Sara woke up from her nap, the two of them went into the yard to play on the big swing set that had been put there by the faeries by them. Mary went to find Hailey and Brian.

When they were seated around the dining room table, a place where Hailey worked on projects the most, she told them that she had something to tell them. And she hoped that they'd not be upset with her.

"I'm not going to London to go to school." Neither of them said anything, but they did have shocked expressions on their faces. And Mary wasn't nearly done yet. "Also, I know when I first came here that I was a little shit and didn't want to call you Mom or Dad, but I want to do that now. I need to do that now. You've both been the best parents to me, and I feel like I've done you wrong in not acknowledging you from the start on how I have come to feel about you."

"Oh, Mary, you've done something that I've never done before. You've rendered your mother speechless." They all laughed, and she hugged them both. Is it something that we said? Or the girls that made you want to stay. I'm all for it myself, but you don't have to stay behind for them. I think we'll do just fine when you're away."

"I want to be their big sister. I have been feeling like that for the last couple of days, what it's like to have siblings. And I have to tell you, I love it. I'm sure they'll get on my nerves, too, but I love those two like they are really my biological sisters. I don't want to miss anything that they do or figure out on their own. I love Hanna's way of cutting to the quick of things. The way she breaks it down so that Sara will understand too. I love the way that they have just accepted everything going on around them without having any kind of trouble with it. She even asked Banny if he'd have to nibble on her too. I love them both so much."

Mary told them, too, that she wanted to protect them when they were out. "Not that I don't think you guys can do it, but they have taken a part of my heart and made it their own, and I want to shield them from every bad thing that comes along. And I know that it will. Just like it did for me."

She'd been with the Tesslers about six months when her father had broken out of jail and come for her. She, like Hanna, had called the police on her father and that had made her a target for him. He'd killed her mother like she was nothing more than a bug, and she had had enough. Now here she was, as happy as she'd never been when living with them. And things in her life were stable too.

Hanna came into the house with Sara sobbing. Whatever had happened had her wanting to find a gun and shoot the person that would dare make one of them cry. But all it turned out to be was that Sara had fallen and scraped her knee. Hanna must have seen something on her face that alarmed her, and she told her to chill out.

"It's just a bump, Mary. Geesh, we get them all the time. I think it's because we're closer to the ground or something. But getting a little bump on our knees is much better than having a fist in our faces. Don't you think?" Mary nodded, so close to crying that she couldn't speak. "What are you gonna do when we get a cold? You're going to drive us crazy, aren't you?"

"Probably." She hugged them both and put a

band aide on Sara's knee. It was nearly healed by then, but Sara had wanted one that had a princess on them, and Mary couldn't turn her down. She was going to make it her mission to find all kinds of bandages to put on scrapes that might come to happen to them.

After their baths that Mom helped them with, they were ready for their story. Brian, or Dad, was going to read to them like he had to her when she was smaller. She wondered when she'd gotten too old to have stories read to her and regretted that too. Mary decided that she was going to be there with them every night for story time. The book he was reading to them tonight was about a stinky cheese man, to the delight of all three of them.

When she made her way to her bed later, she started unpacking the things she'd wanted to take with her when she left. Putting the things back in her room didn't make her sad, but it did make her feel like she had made the right decision. Being a family, that's what she had missed—because she'd been a little shit—having missed as a kid growing up in this house.

Hailey joined her in her room just as Mary was getting into bed. "I came to make sure that you still want to skip London. But I can see that you've already made that decision." Mary told her that she loved being a big sister. "I was the baby in my family. My brother and sister are both older than me. Alex is seven years older, and Sally was about Hanna's age when I was born. They didn't love me like they do now. I guess I was too much of a baby to them."

"I'm really glad that my mom didn't have any more children after me. I missed having any siblings, but I don't think they would have faired well around my father. He was a mean man, and there was no reason for it." Hailey told her that she'd come to realize that most people didn't need a reason to be mean. It was just second nature to them. "I think I figured that out as well. It took me a bit longer, but I think that people, some anyway, take what they want and damn the consequences."

The two of them talked about the upcoming weekend garage sales that the community was holding. Banny and the rest of the kiss would buy a lot of things that they didn't need just to help out families. She loved that about them all. They were never afraid to get their hands dirty when it came to work needing to be done around town. She even got to work when it was needed.

As she watched the moon drift between the stars and trees, she thought of her life and the sudden happy change that she was experiencing. If anyone had asked her even a week ago that she'd be giving up her trip and college education to hang out with a couple of little girls, she would have told them no way. Now she couldn't wait for each day to start to spend with her bigger family. Tomorrow she was going to show them around town, telling people that they were their newest addition to the family. People in town would welcome them as they had her, and she was thrilled about that. Closing her eyes, she let herself drift off.

It was nearly one in the morning when her bed moved. Waking up enough to see what was going on, she was happy that Hanna and Sara were wanting to crawl into bed with her. Making room, enlarging the bed, something that she'd never done before, they were all comfy in ten minutes. Mary could feel the large smile on her face as she went to sleep again. Yes, she thought, she was going to love being a big sister.

Chapter 8

Five years later

Banny was staring off into space when he heard someone snoring loudly. It was his dad. How long he'd been sitting there was anyone's guess. The very fact that he had his head back and snoring made him think it had been a while.

"Dad?" Not only did his dad wake up, but he nearly scared him to death the way he came up out of the chair with not only a knife in his hand but a gun as well. "Christ, Dad? What the hell is going on that you wake up and your first thought is to kill someone?"

"I've not been sleeping well." Banny didn't think that was a good enough reason and told him that. "I know. But I've been having bad dreams about your mother, I mean Hanna. Like horrific ones. The day that she sold me to those men? Well, that's been haunting me a great deal. Mostly because I can't get over the fact that she actually did that. To her mate."

"I think about that as well. How she was able to get around that one law where you can't harm your mate. Much less have them killed. I even talked to Melisandre too. Did you know that she knew her?" Dad told him that he'd not known that. "She told me that the only way that she might have been able to get around that was to have publicly denounced you. Someplace where you could have heard her. Do you remember that?"

"No. I don't remember her—" He could tell that his dad had thought of something. When he frowned and then looked at him with a shocked expression, he knew that he had it. "Right after you were born. She was in the nursery with...oh lord, son, she had a pillow in her hands. She was talking to you, and you were looking up at her. She said...I always thought that I'd misheard her. That she'd never say anything like that to her only son. Hanna said that she disowned you and would never love you. That she was never going to claim you as her own. Then she turned to me and, in the same sing-song voice, said the same to me. She denounced us when you were nothing but an infant, son."

Leaning back in his chair, he thought about what his dad had just told him. In essence, his mother had never wanted him. Had never loved him since the day he'd — hell, he thought, she'd never wanted him in the first place because she'd never wanted his dad. And it hurt him.

All the way to his heart and beyond. When Kelly joined them, a baby in each arm, she handed one of them to Dad and the other to him. His sons. Crying softly to them, he told them that he would never not love them. No matter what they did now or in the future. Hugging Nathan tightly in his arms, he told his son how much he loved him.

As soon as his daughters sat in chairs next to him and hugged him, Banny cried more. He couldn't imagine, not ever in his life, being able to tell his children that he didn't love them. Holding them tightly, perhaps just a little too tight, Jane told him to let her go. She went to her grandda.

"Are you all right, Daddy?" He told Alice that he was all right now that they were all here. "Momma told us that you were having bad thoughts and that we had to come and chase them away. Did we help?"

"More than you can imagine, honey." His little girls were teens now, fifteen, and he couldn't have been more proud of them. His boys, at six weeks old, were named for himself and his father. Bancroft and William Dalton. Using both their names for them had settled all kinds of arguments he'd had with naming them after him. Bancroft Dalton the Fifth. He didn't want to have his kids called a shortened name like Banny if he could help it. Bancroft would be called Croft. A name that he'd come to love since they'd been born.

"Well, that helps me a great deal now." Dad, however, didn't let go of the children. "You know, it's funny really. I have children of my own again. Four little girls that I love to pieces. But holding onto a grandchild? Well, I have to tell you, Banny, there is nothing sweeter. Nothing in the world that can make a man feel like he's done his duty to the world by having a grandchild tell him that they love him."

"I love you, Papaw. With all my heart." Jane looked at her brother in her papaw's arms. "He's not so ugly as he was when he was born. He doesn't look all pinched up and stuff."

Dad laughed, and Jane came to him. When she asked if her sister wanted to go out to the pool, they both left, skipping out of his office as they usually did. Banny looked at his dad. He was still holding Willis in his arms and talking to him. Telling him how lucky he was to have the best momma in the world.

"Hey. What about me? I'm pretty good too." Dad just rolled his eyes at him and continued talking to the baby. "Well, I see how you are. I'll remember that the next time you want me to babysit for you and Bea."

After his dad left, having been able to share lunchtime with the girls, Banny got back to work. He didn't really need to work every day now, and when he did work, he didn't allow distractions to get to him. But with what his dad had said about Hanna, his biological mother, it cut deep within his soul.

"Do you want me to smack you around?" Banny smiled at Kelly. "I will, just so you know. The fucking bitch is gone, left the world. Stop letting some misguided bitch take up your time when she doesn't deserve it."

"She never loved me." Kelly came and sat on his lap. "Never. I can't...it hurts me that she was never anything to me. And I'm only just now thinking of the things that I did to try and get her to love me even a little."

"I know. When I think of the things that she did to try and get you to save her from death, I want to go and find every piece of ash there was from her death and crush them under my heel. I'm just happy that she never got to know the children. There is—never mind. We're not going to go down the what-if road. She's gone. We're happy and parents to incredible children."

"We are at that." When she left him after a quick kiss, he got down to business. Even having as much money as they had, it was hard work to make sure that it kept coming in. Thinking about his buddies, all of them as close to him as real brothers, he wondered what he'd be doing right now without them around.

Remy had married Lizzy not long after meeting her. They had four children, all of them younger than his four. And they were happy. Lizzy, after being raped by several vampires after being kidnapped, had helped a lot of vampires that had had the same thing happen to them. Remy was always there for her when she would be overwhelmed by the stories that the women would have.

He was proud of them both. Remy, like the others, had only accepted his invitation to come here to tell him goodbye. It was in his head to meet the sun and end his life. Now he was his second, making sure that he was safe when he was out and about. Or when there was a conflict that had to be resolved elsewhere. Over the years, it had worked out well for all of them. Even Lizzy. Her life had become meaningful to her again, and she was a bright light in Remy's life now.

There wasn't anything that he could say that would have a person understand the relationship between him and CJ. Donald, her mate, was so laid back, being mated to the queen of faeries, that he wondered at times if anything bothered the older vampire. Banny did laugh at times when CJ would get all riled up, and all Donald would have to do would be to touch his hand to her. Either by taking her hand or simply hugging her. She would calm down so quickly that it was something to see.

He loved them both for their help with the faeries and for keeping the world full of magic too. Because without the magic of the faeries and other creatures in her realm, there would be nothing but dead earth and no humans around. All would die without the magic that she controlled.

Of course, CJ wouldn't agree with him. Simply because she loved to disagree with him at every opportunity she got. Even if she was wrong, she'd argue with him. He would, at times, just get her pissy so that he could laugh at her when she realized what he'd done. Banny didn't do that often, but he did it enough that he would enjoy it immensely.

Clyde and Gracie were wizards. Their magic was stronger than his, and they both knew it. However, he'd never been really afraid of them harming him. He knew, even being immortal, that they could hurt him so that he'd wish for death. But it had never come up for which he was eternally grateful for.

The two of them had made great plans and saw them through to make sure that CJ was safe. Being the queen of faeries would make her a target for almost any other creature. Gracie and CJ were the best of friends. All the women were, but those two had a closer bond than anyone he'd ever encountered before. They also worked hard together. And for that, he couldn't have been happier about.

Banny would only admit to himself how worried he'd been about Brian when he'd first come to visit. He was a good man, but he'd been broke. Not only that, but his parents had been as well. Since he'd been old enough to earn some money, he'd been a good son and made sure that his family had what they needed. It wasn't until he met Hailey that things seemed to turn around for the couple.

He'd given him a job, a construction job that was desperately needed around town. After four short years, not only had Brian taken the company and made it bigger than Banny could have anticipated, he had hired a great many people that were willing to move and take the company further reaching than just Ohio. It had become the largest construction company in the world and had more employees than any other company in the United States.

Hailey still practiced law. She'd become a mentor

to their oldest child, an adopted daughter named Mary, and they both worked with the government on Cybercrimes. As the world grew more dependent on their computers and other devices, it had opened the door to more crimes committed.

Banny found it scary at times the stories that they would tell him about a crime that they'd solved. Even with him being able to use a computer as well as he did, he did oftentimes wonder how they were able to not just track down the criminal but to be able to find where they were hiding in his great big world.

When Kelly told him that she was going out, he finished up his work and closed down his computer. It was family time now, and he was going to enjoy it to the best of his ability. While in the kitchen, fixing dinner for the girls, Brian came to see him. After teasing the girls about their choice for their meal, he sat down and talked to him about his plans. Banny enjoyed this time with Brian as much as he did spending time with Kelly and his kids.

"Hailey and I were in town last night when a call came in about a car accident. There were children involved that needed a safe place." Banny asked him if they were all right. "Yes. There were five of them. Ranging from almost sixteen, she's quick to point out that she's almost old enough to have been driving to four. They were escaping a — well, Banny, one of the worse situations I've ever seen children be in at home. Christ, it makes me physically ill to think of what they had to be living in all the time."

"Tell me about it." He did in great detail. When he finished telling him the horrific conditions that the children were subject to, Banny had to sit down. Again, his heart was taking a hit today. "So they were living with their maternal grandmother, and she was a hoarder. I've heard of people like that. I've never actually met one, but now that you've described a situation for me, I'm very glad that I've not. What do you want me to do for you?"

"The youngest, Billy, had been bitten by a rat. When I went to the house to find them things that they had to leave behind, I just closed the door and left. Whatever they need, they're not going to be getting it from that place. And I saw a rat. Never." Brian shivered and stood up to stretch. Like he needed that before he could go on. "Anyway, I'm going to need some help finding their family. I haven't any idea why they were sent to the grandmother when they have an aunt and uncle that could have taken them in. But then, I'm not in charge of those things. Hailey is fit to be tied. I've never seen her so pissed off."

"I don't blame her, do you?" He said that he didn't. Brian then told him that the others were at his home too. Even Kelly. "She told me she was going out, but I don't remember if she told me where or not. What are they all doing? Plotting?"

"Pretty much. The reason that I need your help. I want to set up a hotline that will help kids like these to be able to call someone to come and get them. I know that we're going to get a lot of calls that will be just kids not liking something that their parents have done, but there really needs to be something where—Jamie, the oldest, stole a car, drove without any knowledge whatsoever where she was going or for that matter how to drive a car because she was looking for a hospital to take her little brother to. That can't be the only solution when something like that happens, Banny. There are so many things that could have gone wrong with this that it's a small wonder that the police are baffled as to what to do with her. She saved her family, but if she'd been in an accident trying to save him, how many lives might have been taken with this? I don't want to leave that to chance. Not again."

"All right. I like that idea. Have you given it much thought on how to make it work? And I have to ask, why didn't she call someone to help her." He said that was the next part. "They had no phone."

"Not only no phone, but there wasn't any running water or any electricity. The place was a dump. It should have been torn down decades ago if you ask me." Banny didn't know how much more of this sort of news he could take. "I'm dumping on you. And I'm sorry. I saw your dad earlier, and he told me what you two had figured out. I'm sorry about that."

"Thank you. I didn't know that Dad was having nightmares about it, but he said that he thought now that he had an understanding more of what Hanna had been about, he thought he could sleep better." Brian said that it would have helped him, too, he thought. "Yes. Well, it helped, and it didn't. But we're getting it figured out. That's the most important part, I believe."

The two of them talked about the planning of

Brian's idea. It was a great one, too, but there were details that needed to be finished before they could make a start on it. Brian wanted to make sure that there was a phone in each household that would take in children because of one reason or another. It wouldn't have worked in the home that the children had been in. Without electricity, the phone wouldn't have been able to charge. So they would need to figure out how to make it work in those situations. It was his opinion that the children should never have been left there in the first place the way the house was, but again, they'd not been in charge of such things.

"I'll work on some more details when I get home. I feel better just talking to you about it." Banny did as well. It was something that he could get behind. When Brian left, Kelly came home soon after. He listened to her as she told him about the conditions that the Wyeth family had had to endure.

~*~

Brian watched the children as they settled into their rooms. He and Hailey had never had any biological children of their own, but they had a hundred or so children in their home over the years. He would admit that he wished for a child of his own, to see Hailey large with child, but they were happy and working toward a goal that they both enjoyed. Keeping children safe.

Hailey met him at the doorway once she put the two youngest in the beds the faeries had set up for them. When he hugged her to him, it was Jamie that came to tell them thanks. That was something that he loved. For the children that they helped knew that they were in a safe and secure home.

"If you don't mind, I'm going to take another shower." He nodded and told her to go ahead. "I don't want to make your bill high. I know that we've all had baths, but I want to feel clean again. All right?"

"I understand. You take a long shower and wash up. There will always be enough hot water for you so long as you stay here." She asked him if they could. "Stay here? I don't know, honey. We have to notify your relatives. And your grandma, who was given custody of you, will have to be evaluated on her ability to care for you guys. There is a great deal of red tape."

"I understand. But what I hear from you is that you'll work on it so that we can stay." She walked away from them, and Brian laughed.

"She's a spitfire. Did I tell you what she told the police when they pulled her over? That she was going to beat them up so that her brother would be taken to the hospital. She's brave too." He agreed with Hailey, and they made their way to the living room. There was a television in the room; however, neither of them watched it alone.

It was for the kids. Not that they watched it much either, but it was there for them. Even though neither he nor Hailey ate all that much food when they didn't have children about, they did have the faeries have things around that would be there for them should they want something in the middle of the night. Or day, for that matter. Brian never wanted a child to go hungry because they didn't know how to cook.

Tomorrow would begin the work on getting the kids what they needed. Shoes, for sure. None of them had been wearing any when they were pulled over. While it was still warm out, if they stayed for any length of time, they'd need coats as well as other warmer things to wear. They'd also need to be evaluated for school. That was one of the hard and fast rules that they had to follow from the state. They had to keep up with their education.

After they'd been seen by a doctor and the youngest set up in the hospital to make sure that the bite didn't cause him any trouble, the kids came home with them. Tonight they'd had a quick meal of sandwiches for them since it had been so late, but they'd have a nice family meal tomorrow that would fill them up with good things. Most of the vegetables would come from his garden out back.

Some of the kids had worked in his garden with him over the years. He thought it important that they learn how to fend for themselves. Planting a few seeds and keeping them watered was a sure way of making sure that they could have something to eat, even if it was only a few carrots. Something that all the kids had enjoyed more than any other seed he planted.

When Hailey dozed off on his chest, he laid her on the couch and got up to go make sure that the faeries knew what was going to be needed tomorrow. The children would all be assigned a faerie that would stay with them when they left their home if they did, but it was up to the faeries to show themselves to them. That had been something that CJ had suggested, as some of the children that had come through their home never got beyond harming others for their needs. And a couple of faeries had been hurt by them.

Just as he was going outside, he felt Mary touch his mind. She was married now. Had a child and was ready to pop the second one. Her words, not his. Mary made him smile with her sassy ways, and her protective nature made him proud to call her his daughter.

"Did you know that the children you have in your home have been with every adoption agency known to man? I'm just putting that out there. I think that Jamie is a good deal like I used to be. Smart mouthed." He asked her if she'd changed somehow over the last few days because he thought she was still smart mouthed. *"Thanks, Dad. That made my day."*

"I didn't mean it as a compliment, Mary." She laughed, and he couldn't help but join her. *"Anyway, no, I didn't know. That's part of my job tomorrow. Finding their relatives."*

"I've had a look. They have an aunt and uncle, as I'm sure you know. They're as bad, if not worse, than the grandma. I guess, as you said a million times, that the apple doesn't fall far from the tree." He asked her what else

she'd been able to find out. Since she worked for child services as well as her job working on cyber crimes, she had the ability to find out all kinds of things for them. *"Jamie has been keeping them together since their parents were killed. They deserved it in the event you were going to ask. I'm not sure that the younger ones remember their parents, but Jamie does. That's why she is so ferocious about keeping them all together. The deadbeat parents tried to sell them off. Why do parents do that? Get knocked up, then sell them off. Stupid if you ask me."*

"Yes, well, *I've seen it plenty of times over the years."* She told him that she was sorry for that. *"Yes, me too. How is Shawn holding up with you about to have another baby? I bet he's no better off now than he was when the first one came along."*

His brother had been mated with Mary. Even though she'd only been a child when he'd met her, Shawn had made sure that she was safe and taken care of. And when she wanted to go to college, he let her go away. Of course, no one ever believed that he didn't hang around the college without her knowledge, but it was what she wanted, and he did it for her. Now that they were married, he'd never seen his brother so happy before.

"*He's better this time by a lot. It could be that I've been threatening him by telling him I was going to tear his dick off, but he's chilling. How about you and Mom?*" He told her the plans that he had with the phone and a place for kids to call. "*Boy, that would be nice to have. Some of the calls that come in are difficult for us to get around to checking out. I'm sure that you'd just send a faerie. But I can't do that. Dad, that's wonderful. Did Mom come up with the idea, and you're taking credit for it? That sounds like something that she'd think of.*"

He laughed. Mary and another foster child they had taken in, Cindy, had been busting his chops since they were children. It hadn't gotten any better either now that they were adults. Brian asked her if she'd heard from her sister recently. The sadness that came through their connection had him sitting down.

"*She's the same old Cindy, Dad. Thinking that no one will love her forever. I wish I could snap my fingers and find her mate for her, but I don't have that ability. Aunt CJ can see bits of her future, but she doesn't seem to be able to find out if Cindy is going to be finding someone to love her. Losing her friends like she did in that accident did her in,*"

I think." Brian said he'd have to have her come home again. To meet the newest members. *"That might work. Maybe I'll come too. That would be fun. Maybe I'll go into labor there, and you can knock Shawn around when he gets antsy. He does that too, and it stresses me out."*

Brian didn't think for a moment that Mary ever got stressed. She was too vocal about things that bothered her. When she was upset, you knew it. However, she never held a grudge, nor did she come back with how something had happened. If you didn't fuck up with her a second time, then it would never be brought up again, and she wouldn't treat you any differently thereafter. He thought of the accident that had taken the lives of nine teenagers five years ago. Cindy had, because of her connection to him and being immortal had been the only one that had survived. Not that she hadn't been beaten up badly.

The bus that they'd been riding on had tried crossing a train track while the lights had been flashing. The kids in the middle of the bus were killed instantly. The others, including the driver, had died from their injuries after being tossed from the bus when it was thrown in the air and hit a second time by the bus.

Cindy had been tossed out, too, but instead of landing in the tracks as most of the other kids had, she was tossed into a tree that was a few hundred yards from the tracks. It had taken them four days to find her. She had spent all her time hanging there, hoping to die. He didn't want to think about her being up there, watching the others being killed or dying like they had been. The guy that she'd been dating at the time he'd been run over by the train when he'd hit the tracks.

"Dad?" Brian told her that he'd been thinking about Cindy. "*Yeah, I do that too. Get lost in her pain. I want so badly to shake her out of this, but I don't — She's calling me. I'll get back to you.*"

Getting things set up for the kids while he waited, he was surprised when both Cindy and Mary contacted him again. Cindy sounded like her old self again. She was not just happy but giddy with it. When she finally calmed down enough to let him know what was going on, he was so happy for his little girl that he wished that she was right there with him.

"*Oh, Dad, he's perfect. And he's a vampire. It was instant, falling in love with him when we met. His name is Daniel Shafer. Oh, I can't wait until you meet him. When he smiled at me from across the room, it was as if every bit of my sadness was suddenly gone. That I knew that for the rest of my life, I'd never have any…oh Dad, I can't wait for you guys to meet him."* He told her that he couldn't either. But did reach out to Banny to let him look into the man's life. *"What are you doing right now? Are you having him checked out? Dad. Why?"*

"Because, my dear child, you are my baby girl no matter what your age. And yes, I'm having him checked out." Banny said that he was a good man with a good family. *"All right. I won't have to stake him. He's past the Banny test."*

They made plans for them to come this weekend. He was as excited as he'd been in a while. When Hailey joined him in the office, he told her what had happened, and of course, she had to call Cindy. He was still smiling when he finished up with the faeries.

Brian thought of himself as a lucky man. More than that, he supposed, he was about as lucky and happy as he'd ever been. When he thought about his life before Hailey and the kids, it was all he could do to believe that it had been his life. Now, there was nothing that he couldn't conquer so long as he had his family at his side.

Life would go on, he knew. There would be ups and downs that they'd deal with. As the years moved on, he knew that there would be changes too. Some he'd like, others he'd not. But with the kiss, his friends and family, he knew he'd never be alone. Or lonely. Brian was glad for his life and was looking forward to the future and what it might bring to him.

AWARD WINNING, BESTSELLING AUTHOR

Kathi Barton, a Pinnacle Book Achievement Award winner and a best-selling author on Amazon and All Romance books, lives in Nashport, Ohio, with her husband, Paul. When not creating new worlds and romance, Kathi and her husband enjoy camping and going to auctions. She can also be seen at county fairs with her husband, an artist and potter.

Her muse, a cross between Jimmy Stewart and Hugh Jackman, brings her stories to life for her readers in a way that has them returning for more. Her favorite genre is paranormal romance, with a great deal of spice. You can visit Kathi online and drop her an email if you'd like. She loves hearing from her fans. aaronskiss@gmail.com.

Follow Kathi on her blog: http://kathisbartonauthor.blogspot.com/